CASTLE AMOR

Erin Caine

Nexus

First published in Great Britain in 1993 by
Nexus
332 Ladbroke Grove
London W10 5AH

A catalogue record for this title is available from the
British Library

ISBN 0 352 32841 X

Phototypeset by Intype, London
Printed and bound in Great Britain by Cox & Wyman
Ltd, Reading, Berks.

This book is a work of fiction.
In real life, make sure you practise safe sex.

CASTLE
AMOR

Contents

1 The Prince

The afternoon sunlight was streaming in through the leaded casement windows, casting playful criss-cross patterns on the bedclothes.

On the bed, Crown Prince Maximilian von Frieden was thoroughly enjoying being instructed in Signora Francesca Delmonico's versatile sexual repertoire. A senior instructress at Friedenheim's Conservatoire of Delicate Arts, Francesca had for several years been one of Prince Maximilian's favourite mistresses. She had such a wicked tongue; such a skilful touch with those long, slender fingers . . .

The Prince gave a long groan of pleasure as she tied the leather thong more tightly about the base of his already-engorged penis.

'It . . . it feels as if it's going to explode!' he cried. 'But it feels wonderful . . . You are a miracle, Francesca. And I don't know what the civilised world would do without the ladies of the Conservatoire – angels of mercy you are, sent out into the world to bring sexual joy and release to all who need it.'

'Hush, hush, my Prince,' whispered Francesca, adjusting the slip-knot on the thong so that it bound the root of his penis as tightly as he could possibly bear. 'You must relax, and let me minister to your delight. For you know that perfect pleasure is the aim of all graduates of the Conservatoire. . . .'

The Prince gave a grunt of satisfaction, and fell back on to the pillows, three fingers of his right hand still buried to the knuckles in Francesca's juicy cunt.

Francesca, too, was enjoying herself enormously. The Crown Prince was such a very apt pupil. He had so often lent himself selflessly to the service of her girls, allowing them to practise their techniques upon his body, and always praising their efforts even when they were gauche and amateurish. And always he managed to climax again and again – especially under Francesca's subtle hands, for she had spent long years studying all the most esoteric sexual arts of both East and West.

The Prince's penis was dancing with eagerness, its swollen head glistening with the beads of clear fluid trickling from the little eye at its tip. It was almost as though the Prince's prick were weeping with gratitude for the pleasure which it was receiving.

Massaging his balls carefully with sweet ointment prepared from frankincense, almond oil and aphrodisiac herbs, Francesca succeeded in teasing Maximilian's prick into even greater rigidity.

'I must have you, Francesca!' he gasped, trails of sweat pouring down his ruddy face as he frigged her with his right hand, hoping to weaken her resistance.

'Patience, patience, my Prince.' Francesca turned him over on to his front, and began to spread the sweet ointment over his buttocks. She worked it skilfully into his flesh with sweeping circular movements that extended from the base of his spine right down to the root of his bollocks.

Gradually, she insinuated her fingers between the Prince's buttocks and eased them apart. The Prince was almost sobbing with frustration now, for he dearly loved to have his mistresses toy with his arse. There was nothing he liked better to fuck one woman whilst another lay atop him, stretching his arsehole with a dildo.

Francesca smoothed the fragrant ointment between Maximilian's buttocks, and into the secret cleft between them, gradually moving closer to his tight little arsehole, which had begun to pulsate with the desire to be filled and gratified.

The Prince was clutching at the pillows now, his knuckles white with the effort of maintaining his self-control. His breath was staccato and hoarse.

Carefully selecting precisely the right degree of pressure, Francesca began to rub the amber rose firmly, making sure that her manicured fingernail teased the Prince's perineum. As she pressed his flesh, he began to make slow copulatory movements, thrusting his buttocks upwards, to receive the full benefit of her exquisitely cruel caresses.

The Prince's throbbing arsehole was so diligent in its efforts that it suddenly swallowed up Francesca's fingertip, engulfing it in warm, secret flesh. Francesca took this as a sign, and wriggled her finger further into him, stretching the walls of his arse with broad, circular movements, and making him cry out with delight.

'Oh . . . oh! I can feel it coming! I fear I'm going to spurt! I can't stop myself . . . !'

Francesca smiled to herself, and promptly slid her left hand down the Prince's secret furrow until it met his balls. Seizing hold of the knot which held the leather thong firmly around the base of his penis, she gave it a further, savage tug, so that a wave of pain surged through him.

3

'Oh, thank you, thank you: you are an angel in human form!'

The Prince, who had suffered a little from premature ejaculation as he grew older, was deeply grateful to Signora Francesca Delmonico, whose skilful ministrations and strict discipline had ensured that he could once again enjoy sex to the full.

This consideration was of the utmost importance in the principality of Friedenbourg, where sex was not only a recreation and a pleasure, but a way of life. The people of Friedenbourg were utterly honest and open about their sexual desires, and it was a common sight to come across couples – and entire families – disporting themselves in unashamed naked frolics, wheresoever they chose.

The government had appointed certain recreational areas, specifically to encourage the citizens to take healthful sexual exercise: Gardens of Earthly Pleasure and Healthful Ease, and Palaces of Sweet Delight – but it was thought acceptable and indeed laudable for individuals and couples to enjoy their own and each other's bodies wherever they chose.

Fucking and buggery were common sights in the streets, and charitable funds had been established to ensure that the poor and the elderly had regular access to professional prostitutes – or Pleasuremaidens, as they were known in Friedenbourg. No form of sexual activity, however bizarre, was regarded as perverse or unacceptable; and people flooded into the principality from the four corners of the globe to sample Friedenbourg's own very special brand of hospitality.

Friedenbourg had become the sexual capital, not only of the Hapsburg Empire, but of the world. Its hotels and colleges and sanatoria attracted disciples of sexuality from all over the world. So it was extremely important its ruler, the Crown Prince Maximilian von Frieden, should be seen to excel at the sexual pleasures and techniques which his subjects were busily exporting to the rest of the civilised world.

Prince Maximilian twisted and turned in delicious agony as Francesca tightened the thong about his prick and bollocks.

'Just a little longer, my darling,' she whispered to him. 'And then I shall allow you to have your first orgasm. The first of many, I promise you . . .'

She resumed her intimate massage of the Prince's buttocks, whilst the index finger of her right hand slid smoothly in and out of his arse like a piston in a well-greased cylinder. This time, as she heard his breathing quickening, she made no attempt to delay his orgasm. In fact, she slipped her left hand under his bollocks and began to squeeze them gently.

With a roar of pleasure, Prince Maximilian von Frieden came to a juddering climax, spurting his abundant semen all over the rose-pink satin sheets which adorned the royal bed.

Afterwards they lay side by side in the afternoon sunlight, chatting while the Prince idly masturbated his mistress.

'Tell me, Francesca: how is the lad faring at the Conservatoire? Have your ladies got him well in hand?'

'Indeed, your Royal Highness – yes, yes . . . a little harder! You know how I love you to masturbate me, my dear Max . . . We have assigned our most skilled and experienced tutors to Prince

5

Albrecht's training. Why, already he has progressed to our course on advanced sexual techniques.'

The Prince's knowing fingers sought out Francesca's throbbing clitoris, and exerted just enough pressure upon it to make her gasp with pleasure, as a trickle of love-juice escaped from her vagina.

'Is that so? Well, well: you must tell me more. I am always anxious to keep up with new developments in sexual technique. My subjects expect it of me, you know. Now – how does this feel?'

The Prince inserted his index finger into Francesca's cunt, and rubbed hard on her clitty with his thumb. Almost instantly, he felt her cunt-juices welling up like some secret underground spring, suddenly brought to the light of day.

'Ah . . . ah . . . I die!' she cried, as fire raged through her loins, and wave upon wave of delicious spasms wracked her cunt.

The Prince beamed, feeling well pleased with himself. Why, the delight he felt at bringing his favourite mistress to orgasm was enough to set his ageing prick twitching into life again.

'Oh Max! You're getting hard again!' cried Signora Francesca, in unfeigned delight. 'Let me help you to get a really nice, hard erection – and then, perhaps, I can show you some of the advanced techniques we have been teaching to Prince Albrecht.'

The Prince nodded his eager assent. This woman really made him feel young again. She had brought virility back to his loins so successfully that he had even been able to reinstate the popular monthly ceremonies in which the Prince rode through the streets of Friedenheim in an open carriage, whilst a citizen – chosen by ballot – knelt before him, sucking his erect penis.

Signora Francesca opened her travelling-bag and took out a collection of small clips, fashioned in pure gold. Seeing the Prince's quizzical expression, she explained:

'These clips are designed to be placed upon selected sensitive areas of the body. Individually, they cause discomfort; but when all six are in place, they set up a field somewhat akin to an electrical circuit of sexual pleasure, and are guaranteed to produce a magnificent and lasting erection.'

Anointing the Prince's body with a sheen of warm lavender oil, she set about fixing the clips, which snapped tight on to his tender flesh, making him gasp with momentary pain. One on either nipple, one nipping the flesh of his perineum, one at the base of his penis, and one on either side of his groin.

A strange and wonderful warmth began to flood through the Prince's body, and he felt blood rushing into the burgeoning shaft of his penis, swelling its tip like the bud of a young sapling in spring.

'It is working, Francesca – I can feel it! It is a miracle of sensual delight!' cried the Prince. 'Come and fuck me, my dear, before this wonderful feeling goes away.'

Francesca shook her head playfully.

'No, no, my Prince. We must wait a few moments for the feeling to grow still stronger – as it most assuredly will – and then I shall show you another little trick which we have developed at the Conservatoire.'

She waited the requisite few moments, and then reached into her travelling-bag once again. This time, she took out a bizarre dildo made of ebony, covered with ornate carvings of mythological beasts, whose massively erect penises made the surface of the dildo extremely irregular.

'I think, my dear Prince, that you will find this most agreeable. The dildo, once placed inside your rectum, will magnify the energy field set up by the golden clips. The effect, during copulation, is most agreeable for both parters.'

The Prince rolled over obediently, and allowed his mistress to insert the dildo into his arse, pushing it home until it was right inside, and the end of it was only just visible within his dilated arsehole.

Then he lay on his back, already groaning with pleasure, and waited for Francesca to mount him.

Francesca's cunt felt like warm, liquid butter around his cock, which seemed to have developed a new, and wonderfully vibrant, life of its own.

Her strong thighs straddled his hips, and her fingers toyed with the golden clips on his nipples as she rode him: at first gently, but then faster, almost recklessly, as though she had forgotten that he was an elderly man, and she, a vigorous woman in her prime.

'It's wonderful, wonderful!' cried the Prince. 'I can feel the semen gathering in my testicles, rising up my shaft. I'm going to come! I'm going to . . . !'

With a cry of ecstasy, he pumped his spunk into Francesca's pulsating cunt, and she fell upon his chest, exhausted.

They lay there in silence for a few moments. Then Francesca raised herself on one elbow, intending to kiss her Prince on the cheek and ask him if he would like her to ride him once again.

But she saw, to her horror, that the Prince's eyes were wide open, staring, unblinking: his lower jaw hung limply in an expression of final, frozen, fatal ecstasy.

Surely the Prince could not be dead . . .

'No!' screamed Francesca, hysterical with grief and remorse. 'What have I done? Speak to me, Maximilian!'

Her screams soon alerted the royal household, and Dieter, the Prince's private groom at Castle Amor, came running to see what was wrong.

He flung the door open on a scene of chaos. The Prince was lying diagonally across his bed, the golden clips still gleaming on nipples and groin, and a trail of semen still running from the tip of his penis. He was not moving. His favourite mistress, Francesca Delmonico, was on her hands and knees beside him, desperately trying to kiss and knead life back into his silent body. She looked up at Dieter imploringly as he entered.

'Please . . . try to do something. The Prince has been taken ill . . .'

Dieter felt for the Prince's pulse, and a shadow crossed his face. He turned to a kitchen boy, who was standing entranced in the doorway.

'Go and fetch the royal physician,' he ordered. 'And send for Prince Albrecht. This is a matter of grave national emergency.'

Prefect Madelon D'Abbeville put down her textbook and stretched out her perfect white limbs on the warm grass.

'I'm tired of revising from books,' she said to her companion, the Honourable Alexandra Fordham. 'How about a little practical revision before class?'

Alex smiled and put down her file of notes.

'You're such a keen student, Madelon. It's no

9

wonder they made you a prefect! Why, I can hardly master the basics of straightforward fucking, and you're already on to the advanced class.' She sighed, knowing that she must try harder if she was going to please her father, Lord Ipswich, and her uncle, Lord Alceston, who had sent her to the Conservatoire in a final attempt to 'improve her social skills'.

Back in England, poor Alex had been more interested in riding to hounds than in learning how to fuck; and her uncle realised that he must act quickly if she were not to become a social outcast. The Conservatoire of the Delicate Arts was Alex's only chance to become a sexual sophisticate.

'Will you help me to learn what I need to know, Madelon?'

'Of course I will, Alex. You know, you worry about it all far too much. Just relax, and I'll go over the theory again. Then we'll try the practical.'

The notes on mutual masturbation were clearly illustrated with diagrams which the girls had copied down in class, yet still young Alex had difficulty in grasping the intricacies of the technique.

Finally, in despair, Madelon put down her book and announced:

'It's no use trying to explain it: I shall have to show you. Come and sit beside me – that's right, hitch up your skirts and tuck them into your belt, as I have done with mine. Now, doesn't it feel good to have the spring sunshine on your cunny? I'm glad to see that you have followed Matron's advice and discarded your knickers – they really are so unnatural and so unhealthy, you know! And remember that a graduate of the Conservatoire must be ready at all times to obey the dictates of her own and others' lusts: if you are wearing those great ugly cotton bloomers, how on earth can you embrace a life of spontaneity? Now, Alex: what is the school motto?'

'Perfect pleasure,' replied Alex brightly, much cheered by the tender kisses her friend was bestowing on her nipples, through the flimsy fabric of her summer blouse, and by the warm sun's caresses on her tender cunt-lips.

'Then remember that motto, and simply copy what I do,' replied Madelon, her finger delving deep into Alex's sandy-coloured pubic hair, and teasing and tugging at it so that Alex's cunt grew quite wet with excitement. 'Yes, that's it, my dear Alex: wind my pubic hair around your fingers so that it pulls a little – not too much, or you'll hurt me. That's right – just tug at it gently. See: my clitty is swelling already, it longs so for your touch!'

Encouraged by her friend's kind words, Alex determined that she would excel at the exercise; and as Madelon gently parted her cunt-lips, she followed suit, opening up the gate to Madelon's secret garden.

'Oh, Madelon – you have the fingers of an angel!' sighed Alex, as the prefect began to work away diligently at her clitty. 'I shall come long before I bring you to your climax.'

'No you shan't!' laughed Madelon, abandoning for a moment her friend's clitty and directing her attentions to Alex's exploration of her own cunt. 'Here – let me move your fingers for you – slow, circular movements at first; just the lightest of touches, to tease my little rosebud into wakefulness . . . and then you can begin to press a little harder, and move your fingers more quickly as you feel my cunt grow wetter. Ah . . . Alex! That is exquisite. Now, see if you can carry on without me to help you.'

Madelon found she was almost losing control of herself; for Alex had truly learned her lesson well, and Madelon's cunt-juices were flowing abundantly, glistening on Alex's diligent fingertips. Taking a deep breath to regain her composure, Madelon set to work once more on Alex's clitty, sliding her index finger inside Alex's cunt, the better to judge and control her pleasure.

'Why, Alex!' she cried. 'You are so tight! Why, a man might think you were still a virgin.'

Alex blushed crimson with shame. Panting with the mounting excitement in her clitty, she gasped:

'I was still a virgin until my sixteenth birthday, a few days before I came to the Conservatoire. My father was appalled when he found out. He had to send me to his valet and gardener to have me fucked and buggered – otherwise, Frau Kässler would have refused to accept me as a pupil. So you see, dear Madelon, unlike you I am a very unpromising student.'

Madelon laughed. 'Silly girl! Can't you feel how excited you're making me? Slide your finger deeper into my cunt – there: can't you feel the cunt-juice flowing round your finger? I don't get wet for just anyone, you know.'

'I . . . I don't think I can last much longer, Madelon,' gasped Alex, feeling an inexorable tide of pleasure rising up through her loins.

Skilfully, Madelon eased off her ministrations just a little, to give her time to catch up with her friend.

'Not so fast, Alex! Remember what Signora Francesca always says: the greatest pleasure is always the longest in coming. I'm not going to let you come until I know you're really going to enjoy it. I want you to have a really wonderful orgasm.'

Taking her hands from Alex's cunt for a moment, Madelon leant across and unbuttoned Alex's school blouse, which was made from the finest, softest, white cotton lawn, cut high at the neck, as was the fashion with ladies of distinction all over Europe; but so diaphanous as to render it almost superfluous.

'I am so glad to see that we have persuaded you away from those terrible stays you were wearing when first you came here!' giggled Madelon, recalling the staid little girl who had arrived at the Conservatoire, so modestly turned out that it might have been her first day at a convent school. 'You have such promising breasts.'

She bent to kiss them, taking each perfect pink nipple in turn into her greedy mouth, and rolling it around upon her skilful tongue.

'Oh Madelon, Madelon! No more – or I shall surely come!'

Madelon gave Alex's nipples a final kiss, and then unbuttoned her own blouse.

'It is your turn to kiss me,' she smiled.

Alex gazed with unbounded admiration upon Madelon's impressive breasts. She really did have the most wonderful figure. Madelon had no need of stays, for her waist was naturally tiny, and her hips naturally rounded and womanly. Gloriously full, firm breasts soared above a taut belly, their hard pink nipples pointing heavenwards, as though receiving angelic inspiration. Like many of her peers at the Conservatoire, Alex was quite besotted with her mentor.

With trembling fingers, she began to stroke Madelon's breasts.

'Don't be so timid,' advised Madelon. 'Just do whatever you would like to be done to you.'

Summoning up all her courage, Alex pinched Madelon's nipples between finger and thumb, and was rewarded with a gasp of unfeigned delight. Encouraged, she bent down and began to suck at a nipple, enjoying the exercise so much that she scarcely noticed how much faster Madelon was breathing, and how much wetter her cunt was becoming beneath her untried fingers.

'My dear Alex, let me rub your clitty a little harder,' gasped Madelon. 'For I fear my own crisis is almost upon me.'

Obediently, Alex spread her legs a little wider, and Madelon delivered the *coup de grâce* to her throbbing clitty.

Squealing with unashamed delight, the two girls came together to the peak of orgasm, and collapsed together on to the warm, green grass.

They lay there for a while, playfully stroking each other's bodies, whilst the warm sunshine soaked into their naked flesh and awoke new and wonderful stirrings of youthful desire.

Suddenly, a distant sound floated towards them from across the playing-fields, filtering into their pleasant day-dreams.

'The bell!' exclaimed Madelon, scrambling to her feet and fastening her grass-stained blouse. 'Hurry up, Alex, or we'll be late for Signora Delmonico's class!'

Frau Irmgard Kässler rose from her chair to greet the new arrivals: a rather nervous young girl with long, blonde plaits, and a distinguished middle-aged man with a sandy-coloured beard – presumably her father.

'Ah, Monsieur Desfarges; you have brought your

charming daughter with you, I see. I hope you had a pleasant journey.'

The man bowed, and kissed Frau Kässler's hand. 'Thank you, yes. My daughter Florence was so excited at the prospect of joining your illustrious academy that she insisted I bring her, even on this preliminary visit. And if I may say so, my dear Frau Kässler, the journey was all the more pleasant for making your acquaintance at the end of it. You have the most agreeable breasts, and I believe I should greatly enjoy fucking you.'

'Ah, Monsieur!' laughed the Headmistress. 'I see that you have already thoroughly entered into the spirit of our quaint Friedenbourg customs. And, if I might remark upon it, I see that the front of your trousers bulges most promisingly, and I should be delighted to fuck with you. Fucking is such an hospitable way of greeting one's guests. If you would be kind enough to unbutton your trousers and take out your prick, we can begin immediately.'

Monsieur Desfarges cast an anxious glance in the direction of his young daughter, who was looking on in saucer-eyed fascination.

'Should I perhaps ask young Florence to leave us . . . ?'

'Good heavens, no, Monsieur! After all, are you not seeking the most liberal of educations for your daughter? It is only fitting that she should be swiftly initiated into the customs of the Conservatoire.'

She turned to Florence, and beckoned her over.

'Come, child. Unbutton your father's trousers, and take out his prick, there's a good girl. A good daughter should always be helpful to her father.'

Florence obeyed, her hands trembling as she fumbled with the buttons and reached inside for her father's burgeoning member. She pulled it out delicately, almost as though she were handling some fragile, injured bird she was terrified of hurting.

'Hurry up, child, we haven't got all day. Can't you see your father is anxious to fuck? Why, one might even think you had never seen a prick before! Now, rub his shaft, so that it's nice and hard.'

At first timidly, and then with greater confidence as she saw the flesh stiffen at her touch, Florence began to masturbate her father's prick. Monsieur Desfarges watched with mounting excitement and an enormous feeling of paternal pride as his daughter ministered with increasing skill to his sexual needs.

'That's it, my girl,' said Frau Kässler, approvingly. 'Run your fingers lightly over the tip, to spread the wetness evenly. That will give him more pleasure. Now then, Monsieur, are you ready for the fray?'

'I believe I am, Frau Kässler.'

'Then come, child, and guide your father's prick into my cunny,' commanded the imperious Head-mistress, bending forward across her desk and hoisting up her skirts, presenting a very fine pair of white buttocks for her guests' appreciation.

Monsieur Desfarges positioned himself behind Frau Kässler, and pulled apart her buttocks, revealing an agreeably tight little arse and a dripping cunt fringed by glossy black curls. The valiant Florence seized hold of his cock, and manoeuvred it into place. Her father reached round and grabbed hold of Frau Kässler's large, soft breasts, and pulled himself into her, sighing with pleasure as her warm, wet flesh enfolded him.

Frau Kässler thrust backwards, taking the Frenchman's shaft deep into her belly.

'On your knees, girl, and lick your father's balls,'

she urged Florence; and the girl obeyed, now beginning to get the idea of this novel game. She pulled her father's trousers and underpants down on to his hips, so that his balls sprang free and she could encircle them with her eager tongue.

At the first touch of her tongue, her father's balls tensed with delight, and he gasped encouragement: 'Good girl, Florence, harder, harder!'

He thrust into Frau Kässler with all the enthusiasm of a starving man for a hearty meal, and she took hold of his right hand and guided it to her cunt.

'Rub my clitty, Monsieur: and you and I shall come together!'

How surprised and delighted was young Florence when, with cries of mutual pleasure, her father and her future headmistress came together, pressing their loins together in a final fusion of fulfilment. And how amazed to see her father's prick emerge, glistening with drips of pearly-white fluid, as it emerged from Frau Kässler's cunt.

Arranging her skirts and tidying her hair, Frau Kässler settled herself back in her armchair.

'That was most pleasing, Monsieur Desfarges. I hope to enjoy fucking with you again before you leave Friedenbourg. And now, we must discuss your daughter's application to join the Conservatoire of Delicate Arts. You have done well, Florence. Off you go, child, and wait in the outer office. The tutors will talk to you about some of the exciting amenities which the school has to offer.'

Regretfully, Florence went through the side door into the outer office, where two of the tutors were engaged in a little extra-curricular foreplay, in which they invited her to join them.

When the door had closed behind Florence, Frau Kässler turned to her father.

'Now then, Monsieur Desfarges. You have read our prospectus, and schedule of termly fees?'

He nodded.

'As you can see, my daughter Florence is most eager to join your illustrious academy, and I for one am behind her every step of the way. Are we not living in a modern world with its own values and customs? Have we not recently entered a new century, with all its exciting challenges? I am most anxious that Florence should receive a liberal education in all the sexual arts, in line with my own beliefs. As you know, her late mother was a former pupil of the Conservatoire, and I always found her an excellent companion in the bedchamber – as did my many friends and business colleagues, whom she so skilfully entertained at my request.'

'Well,' said Frau Kässler, 'I have had a chance to observe your daughter at our fucking, and I must say that I feel she has great potential. Obviously there is the full physical examination for her to undergo, but I am confident that she would make a creditable pupil. However, I am a little worried that she seems lacking in experience. What was the date of her first fucking?'

Monsieur Desfarges looked perplexed.

'Her first fucking? I don't understand.'

'You are, I take it, aware of our regulations? We do not, under any circumstances, admit virgins as students at the Conservatoire.'

Monsieur Desfarges's face fell.

'I had hoped to have her fucked by now,' he sighed. 'And she is eager enough to lose her virginity. But alas, my business has been so busy that

I have not had the time to arrange a meeting with some suitable young man . . .'

The Headmistress looked at him sternly over the top of her horn-rimmed glasses. 'I'm sorry, Monsieur Desfarges, but rules are rules.'

'Then what am I to do?'

Frau Kässler smiled.

'Have no fear, Monsieur; this type of problem does arise from time to time, and I have made provision for it. Friedenbourg is a civilised nation. True, in some of the outlying areas tradition is strong, and young peasant girls are still first-fucked by their fathers, brothers or uncles; but in general the more refined classes send their daughters to a sexual initiator for the first fucking. If you would care to come through to the outer office with me, I will provide you with a list of men I have approved for the defloration of virgins. I have personally fucked all of them, and can testify to their efficacy and excellent background.

'I shall of course be present at her first fucking, and you need have no fear that she will come to any harm. And afterwards, Monsieur Desfarges, perhaps you would like to fuck with me again? The weather is so fine that you might like to join me at the Pleasure-Ground of Sweet Delights?'

Desfarges gave a little bow. 'I should be honoured, Frau Kässler.'

Madelon and Alex sat side by side in the stuffy classroom, and heartily wished that they could be out in the fresh air again, practising what they had learned on each other, or perhaps strolling through the streets of Friedenheim, enjoying a casual and pleasant fuck with some passing stranger.

Signora Francesca Delmonico seemed strangely distracted today, as she took the class through their tongue exercises.

'Pay attention, girls!' she exclaimed. 'It is so very important that you perfect your skill in these exercises; otherwise, your tongues will remain short and weak, and you will never be able to give your partners full satisfaction.'

But her heart did not seem to be in her teaching. A subdued whispering rippled around the class. Could the unofficial rumours from Castle Amor be true? Could Signora Francesca – renowned throughout the principality as the Prince's favourite mistress – really have exhausted him so much with her love-making that he had had to take to his bed for a few days' rest?

The girls regarded Signora Francesca with a new-found respect. Since perfect pleasure was the aim of all Conservatoire students, to have pleasured a partner to the point of complete physical collapse was the ultimate accolade.

'Unfasten your blouses, girls; and practise using your tongues on each other's breasts.'

The girls were just beginning to pleasure each other when the door of the classroom burst open, and the Head Girl, Diana von Sturmbein, rushed breathlessly in.

'News from the Castle!' she cried, quite forgetting that she was interrupting an important lesson. 'Prince Maximilian is dead – he collapsed whilst fucking, and passed away a few hours later.'

The classroom was in an uproar. So Signora Francesca had not only exhausted the Prince – she had hastened his demise!

'It was an honourable death,' commented

Madelon. 'After all, it is the goal of all true-born Friedenbourgians to die whilst fucking.'

'And there is yet more news!' continued Diana. 'His son, Prince Albrecht, cannot accede to the throne because he is not married. Before he can be crowned, he must find himself a wife! And there is to be an open contest to find Prince Albrecht a bride. Any girl resident within the Principality of Friedenbourg may enter!'

Madelon and Alex exchanged meaningful glances.

'I've always wanted to fuck Prince Albrecht,' murmured Madelon, her nipples stiffening in eager anticipation.

2 The initiation

'Don't look so nervous, my dear,' Frau Kässler chiv-vied Florence Desfarges, as they climbed the stairs to Herr Zimmerman's rooms. 'He is a gentleman of impeccable pedigree, and he fucks beautifully. You will thoroughly enjoy your first fucking, I assure you. Now – have you taken the herbal drink which Matron prepared for you?'

Florence nodded.

'Excellent. It will relax you, and also ensure that there are no . . . foolish complications. Fucking should be entirely pleasurable, with no thought of unfortunate consequences.'

They reached the third-floor landing, and stood before a heavy oak door beside which was a polished brass plaque. It read: FRANZ ZIMMERMAN: SEXUAL INITIATOR.

Frau Kässler rang the bell, and after a few moments the door was opened by a pretty girl in a tight dress of yellow muslin, cut very low at the bodice. She was clearly wearing no underbodice or petticoats, for her hard brown nipples and dark pubic hair showed clearly through the fabric. Such light and attractive clothing was both practical and extremely fashionable in the chic city of Frieden-heim.

'Ah, Frau Kässler – how charming to see you again!' exclaimed the young lady. 'And how deliciously firm your breasts are: may I kiss them?'

Charmed by such a welcome, Frau Kässler nodded, and submitted to allowing the lass to unbutton her bodice and kiss the soft, white flesh of her large bubbies. Her nipples hardened beneath such a delicate, exquisite touch, and the Headmistress smiled.

'My dear girl, you have such a practised and agreeable touch. Did you perhaps study under Professor Baumgarten, in Stuttgart?'

'Why, how on earth did you guess?'

'You have precisely that degree of lasciviousness, mingled with exactness of touch, which the Professor instils in all his students. And, if I may say so, you have a wonderfully plump backside, and after we have contracted our business with Herr Zimmerman, I should find it most agreeable to finger-fuck you and lick out your arsehole.'

The girl in the yellow muslin dress blushed with pleasure to hear such a compliment from the lips of Frau Kässler herself, and quickly ushered the Headmistress and her charge into Herr Zimmerman's waiting room.

It was a large and sumptuous room, with a deep carpet of soft, velvety pink and elegant Regency-striped wallpaper: the very epitome of comfort and relaxation. It reminded Florence of a rather exquisite bedroom. The furnishings were tasteful, expensive and most unusual.

The walls were lined with comfortable armchairs, and beside each one stood a small side-table, bearing an array of bizarre objects. Florence reached out and picked one up, feeling its smooth surface wonderingly. It was a life-size model of a penis, carved from smoothest alabaster, and its glossy tip simply begged to be stroked, kissed, licked. Florence blushed crimson as she wondered what it would feel like to have it inside her, as she had seen her own father placing his penis inside Frau Kässler.

'Don't be embarrassed, child,' chaffed the Headmistress. 'These little playthings are provided for you to touch and toy with. Do you like the model of a cunt? It is very lifelike, is it not?'

Wide-eyed and trembling with excitement, Florence experimented with the two toys and soon discovered that she could slide the penis into the cunt. This was so agreeable a diversion that it was quite some time before Florence tired of it and cast her eyes round the room to see what other amusements Herr Zimmerman had provided.

The walls were lined with erotic pictures from every period of history and every part of the world: brightly coloured Persian prints depicting men with huge penises and their sweet, submissive womenfolk; Indian illustrations from the Kama Sutra; little-known works by the Impressionists, depicting the French bourgeoisie fucking with impeccable style and decorum; and even lewd illustrations from medieval illuminated manuscripts.

But the most interesting of all the playthings were the two life-sized marble statues, one male and one female, which stood on either side of the fireplace, holding up the mantelpiece.

The woman had a magnificent body: lithe and yet feminine, softly curving and infinitely inviting. She was standing with thighs wide apart, and Florence discovered, to her delight, that the statue was more accurate than she had imagined – for her finger slid easily up into the marble figure's cunt.

Next, she turned her attentions to the male statuette, whose massive, upward-soaring penis was so beautiful that Florence could not help wondering what it would feel like to sit herself upon it, and feel it sliding up into her cunt, slicing through her virgin flesh like a knife through butter.

As she was contemplating this delightful prospect, under the watchful eye of the Headmistress, the door opened and in walked the girl in the yellow dress.

'Herr Zimmerman is ready for you now,' she announced. 'If you'd like to follow me . . .'

Florence and Frau Kässler followed the girl down a short corridor into another room, smaller than the first but equally sumptuously decorated. The centrepiece of the room was a rather elegant consulting-couch, covered with gleaming white satin sheets. The assistant signalled to Florence to undress and lie down on the couch. A couple of chairs were lined up against the wall, and Frau Kässler took a seat.

After a few moments, a connecting door opened and in walked Herr Franz Zimmerman, a tall, bearded man of perhaps thirty-five years, with twinkling blue eyes and a very prominent bulge in the front of his trousers. He greeted Frau Kässler as he would an old friend:

'My dear Irmgard!' he cried. 'Your breasts are lovelier even than I remembered, and I long to seize and kiss their magnificent flesh.'

'You are too kind, my dear Franz,' replied Frau Kässler. 'I, for my part, would very much like to drink down your cock-juice, as I have so often done in the past. But alas, I am here on business, with this young lady, Mademoiselle Florence Desfarges. I fear the poor girl is yet a virgin!'

Herr Zimmerman shook his head sadly.

'Why, the poor lass must be sixteen, if she's a day! It's a crime to let such ripe young flesh go untasted. I had my own daughters properly fucked as soon as they were big enough to take a cock, and Lord knows they'd been licking each other's clitties since they were tiny babes in arms. Still, we cannot but marvel at the barbaric customs of other nations, and be profoundly grateful that here in Friedenbourg we have the freedom to enjoy sexual pleasures to the full. Now then, my little French miss, what is it that I can do for you?'

Florence gazed up at the darkly handsome Herr Zimmerman, and felt an unaccustomed warmth spreading through her virgin loins.

'Frau Kässler says that I must be fucked, or she will not accept me as a pupil at the Conservatoire. Will you fuck me, please, Herr Zimmerman?'

The initiator laughed, and began to get undressed.

'Of course I shall, my sweet. Now, do you know the procedure here? I must first empty my loins by masturbation, so that when I fuck you I can last long enough to pleasure you – for, in truth, my cock is so hard at the delectable sight of you that I fear I should come within seconds if I were to enter you now. You may wish to masturbate, too, my dear: an orgasm will help you to relax.'

Seeing Florence's blank expression, Herr Zimmerman realised the incredible truth.

'Have you never masturbated, child? Never played with your clitty?'

Florence shook her head, sadly.

'I have touched myself sometimes,' she replied.

'But although I excited myself, I have always ended up feeling terribly frustrated and not knowing what to do next.'

Herr Zimmerman unbuttoned his trousers and stepped out of them. He was wearing no undergarment, and his prick sprang out eagerly, its tip already glistening with the anticipation of pleasure. Florence noted with surprise and great curiosity that Herr Zimmerman's cock had been pierced, and a thin gold ring had been inserted into the end.

Seeing her confusion, the initiator reassured her:

'Have no fear, sweet Florence. The ring is there only to give both of us greater pleasure. I think you will find the sensation most agreeable. And now, you must masturbate for me. My assistant will show you what to do. Helga!'

The door opened, and the girl in the yellow dress returned.

'Ah, Helga. Kindly sit yourself down on that chair over there, facing Mademoiselle Desfarges, and show her exactly what she should do to masturbate.'

Helga readily pulled up her skirts and sat down in front of Florence, her legs wide apart and her dark-fringed cunt-lips clearly displaying the treasures within.

'This is my cunny-hole,' began Helga, inserting the tip of her finger into the pink wetness. 'I sometimes put my finger in there when I masturbate. And this is my clitty: see how hard and pink it is? It is throbbing with desire, for it knows what I am going to do next. Can you find your clitty, Mademoiselle?'

Awkwardly propped up on a pile of pillows, Florence explored her womanhood. First the cunny: yes, that was easy enough. But her finger would not slide in as far as Helga's had done, for she was still a virgin, and it hurt her to press against the thick membrane of her maidenhead.

But where was her clitty? Could this be it? No, it could not be, for she felt no special sensation. Or this? Ah, yes! An enormous surge of pleasure washed over her as her finger pressed incautiously upon the sensitive little pink button.

'I see that you have found it, Mademoiselle!' smiled Helga. 'Now, scoop up some of the wetness in your cunny-hole, and smooth it over your clitty – yes, that's right, like that. You will find it makes masturbation so much more agreeable if your clitty is wet. Now, touch your nipple with your left hand – pinch it gently . . . does that feel good? And then begin to rub your clitty with a gentle, circular motion . . .'

Florence watched the girl masturbate in front of her, and tried to follow suit. She was almost weeping with frustration – her tension and desire were growing, and yet she could not quite find the way to bring herself the final, ultimate, infinite pleasure.

'Here, girl: let me show you!' exclaimed Frau Kässler, finally losing patience and crossing the room to help her. She seized hold of Florence's errant finger, and placed it once again upon her clitty, this time guiding it so that there could be no doubt of the final outcome.

Florence's eyes grew wide with astonishment and delight as she felt her first-ever orgasm beginning.

'I . . . I . . . what is happening to me, Frau Kässler? It feels so wonderful, and so terrible! I fear I am going to die!'

And with a shriek of pleasure, she fell back on to the couch as the Headmistress's expert fingers prolonged her crisis to the utmost.

As Florence lay panting on the satin sheets, Herr Zimmerman stood over her and began to masturbate with practised skill. He cradled his balls in his left hand, gently squeezing them to stimulate the flow of semen; whilst with his right he pumped his shaft up and down, demonstrating to his pupil exactly how a man could bring himself pleasure.

Though he tried to prolong the exercise for the benefit of Florence's education, his crisis was, as he had predicted, swift in coming. With a sigh of resignation, he gave his shaft a few final strokes, and Florence looked on in amazement as she saw the pearly-white fluid oozing from the tip of his penis and flooding his palm.

'And now,' announced Herr Zimmerman, wiping the semen from his hands with a soft embroidered towel, 'I believe we are ready to begin. As you can see, my dear Mademoiselle Desfarges, my penis is already returning to rigidity, and I am ready to take your virginity. Do you feel that you have been sufficiently prepared for the experience?'

Florence nodded vigorously.

'Matron has explained it all to me. She gave me a funny-tasting herbal drink, and now I feel so very excited! And I helped my father fuck Frau Kässler, so I think I know what happens.'

'Part your legs, my dear,' instructed the Headmistress, 'so that Herr Zimmerman can get a good look at your cunt.'

Florence did so, and Herr Zimmerman's assistant handed him a pot of something oily and fragrant.

'This is the ointment we use to prepare the area,' explained Herr Zimmerman, spreading it all over Florence's cunt. 'I think you will find it both soothing and . . . stimulating.'

The feeling was like fire and ice, inextricably mingled. The ice soothed her, almost numbed her, but always the fire was there, teasing and tormenting and awakening flesh to the promise of a savage pleasure she had never known before.

Herr Zimmerman climbed on to the couch and knelt between Florence's thighs, drawing up her knees around him. Helga stood beside Florence, gripping her hand tightly for moral support.

'It may hurt a little,' Herr Zimmerman told Florence. 'But soon the pain will give way to the most exquisite pleasure.'

He lay upon her belly, and Florence felt his hardness pressing against the tiny, tight opening to her womanhood. How could such great hardness ever find its way into such tight, unyielding flesh? She felt fear, and yet she knew she must not draw back now. She would be a pupil at the Conservatoire! She would become one of their most illustrious graduates!

'I am ready, Herr Zimmerman,' she whispered. 'Please take me quickly. Do not be afraid to hurt me.'

The ointment eased the passage a little, but Herr Zimmerman's prick was large and Florence's cunny-hole tiny and extremely tight, for all the juices that had flowed from it. The first entrance of his penis felt like a burning rapier-thrust, and Florence could not suppress the tears that sprang to her eyes.

'Courage!' cried out Frau Kässler.

And with the second thrust, he was inside her. It felt for a moment as though he were splitting her in two, but then the discomfort began to ease off and another, more insidious feeling began to take over.

A spreading warmth overcame Florence as her

initiator thrust into her again and again, with long, satisfying strokes. She forgot the pain, the fear, the apprehensiveness, and began to glimpse the pleasure that she was about to experience.

'Fuck me, fuck me, Herr Zimmerman! I am going to be a woman . . . I am going to come!'

As his prick stretched her cunt and his downy bollocks slapped against her backside, Florence felt her existence reduced to the simple truth of her cunt: her pulsating, throbbing, glistening, yearning cunt; and her clitty that cried out for the ultimate fulfilment.

Herr Zimmerman was agreeably surprised as he felt Florence's fingers slide between their thighs and begin to toy with his balls. This innocent young Mademoiselle with the blonde plaits and the doe eyes was, it seemed, an extremely quick learner . . .

With groans of satisfaction they came together, Florence's cunt drinking in Herr Zimmerman's spunk as though it were the very elixir of eternal youth.

When he climbed off her, Florence saw with enormous pride that the white satin sheets were soaked with her blood, mingled with the pearly stickiness of Herr Zimmerman's semen. These sheets, neatly folded and presented to her, were to be her very first souvenir of Friedenbourg.

'Congratulations, my dear!' exclaimed Frau Kässler. 'Now we can welcome you as a pupil at our academy. Thank you, Herr Zimmerman – you have done your job well, as always. I trust that the labour was not too onerous. Perhaps you would like to meet later, in the park, for a fuck?'

'I will meet you on the Boulevard of Heavenly Delights at seven, my dear Irmgard,' replied Zimmerman, wiping the blood from his penis. 'And my dear Mademoiselle Desfarges, rest assured that I shall be delighted to fuck you at any time'.

It was a joyful Florence Desfarges who made her way to the school that afternoon, to attend her very first classes at the Conservatoire.

Alex sighed as she watched the posters going up in the main square outside Friedenheim Town Hall.

'Oh Madelon, I'd love to enter – but what chance have I?'

Madelon smiled.

'Of course you have a chance, Alex – you have such a wonderfully aristocratic background. It's I who have no chance. I'm just an ordinary bourgeoise, the daughter of a Swiss banker.'

A large crowd of young women had gathered in the square to read the details of the contest to find a wife for Prince Albrecht, ruler-elect of the principality of Friedenbourg. All were anxious to know how to enter, and perhaps become the next Crown Princess of Friedenbourg. In addition to the girls from the Conservatoire, there were plump and delectable peasant-girls from the outlying farms, ladies-in-waiting from Castle Amor, simple serving-girls and mill-girls, and all the cream of Friedenbourgian society.

'The contest is to have two stages,' read Alex. 'After preliminary interviews there will be a selection of eight finalists. The final contest will take place at the Castle, where the finalists will be required to perform a routine of sexual ingenuity for the benefit of, and involving, Crown Prince Albrecht. Oh dear, Madelon: it all sounds very daunting!'

'I'm sure our teachers will guide us through it,'

replied Madelon. 'And now, how would you like to go for lunch and then have a stroll in the Garden of Earthly Pleasures? It's a beautiful day, and there are bound to be lots of interesting people there.'

'I'm sorry, Madelon – I have to get back to the Conservatoire. Señor Jerez is giving me some extra tuition in fellatio. But we'll be together again this evening. I must rush – but I'll see you at supper!'

Ah well, thought Madelon. I might as well go and have lunch in one of the cafés on the Boulevard of Heavenly Delights.

She strolled out of the square and turned left into Bettstrasse, where the weekly street-market was held. Traders from all over the principality gathered each Wednesday in Friedenheim to sell their wares, and a charming array of stalls had been set out along the street.

Madelon examined some of them as she passed. An old woman was sitting beside the kerb with a basket of intricately carved wooden dildos, whilst her daughter offered to display their efficacy between the thighs or buttocks of any passer-by who might feel the need of their relief. A group of young women were gathered round a stall specialising in neat little gold rings for the nipples and clitoris.

Madelon smiled to herself as she recalled the day when she had first had her clitty pierced. How frightened she had been! And how foolish to have had such groundless fears – for, though the pain of the needle had made the tears spring to her eyes, the discomfort had been almost instantly replaced by a feeling of the most tremendous excitement.

She had been a mere slip of a girl at the time, rather unsophisticated, and only moderately skilled in fucking; and this newfound surge of sexual desire had quite driven her to distraction. Her appetite for sexual pleasures – always hearty – grew so prodigious that, within three months of her arrival at the Conservatoire, Madelon surprised and delighted her parents by being appointed a prefect.

She moved closer to the stall and pressed her thighs tightly together, still thrilled by the sensation of the ring which pierced her so-sensitive clitoris. As a rule, Madelon favoured a plain gold ring, though occasionally she wore one of the more ornate trinkets which had been devised to thrill both partners during intercourse.

Like all senior pupils at the Conservatoire, she carried with her a range of devices to stimulate the clitoris and penis; for mutual gratification was a vital element of Friedenbourg's unique sexual code. It was considered the worst of all insults to take one's own pleasure without attending to the intimate delight of one's partner, however transient and casual the meeting might be.

Madelon took up her place among the semi-circle of spectators who had gathered to watch a young peasant-girl having her clitoris pierced. Her father was looking on, offering encouragement to his timorous daughter, who was staring in undisguised terror at the stallholder and his fine, sharpened needle.

'Have no fear, dear Fräulein,' soothed the stallholder, applying a little rose-scented cold-cream to the girl's clitty, and rubbing it to ease her into pleasurable relaxation. 'You shall soon experience the most exquisite enjoyment. See: I have had my penis and scrotum pierced in three separate places; and it gives me the greatest joy to feel the thrill as each little ring is caressed by the warm folds of a cunt, or a lad's moist pink tongue.'

The girl's legs were wide apart, the skirts of her rough linen gown pulled up around her waist; and Madelon could not suppress a shiver of anticipatory excitement as she looked at the pink freshness of her cunt, and the hard moist pearl that the stallholder was still rubbing with cold-cream.

The stallholder's assistant went round the crowd of onlookers, handing out pfennig dildos so that the spectators could pleasure themselves whilst watching. It was such an agreeable spectacle for a warm summer's afternoon that dozens of Friedenbourg's citizens had flocked to the stall in their lunchhour.

Madelon paid her penny and accepted the simple wooden dildo, still fragrant with the cunt-juices of its last owner. She hoisted up her uniform skirt, and sat down on a convenient orange-box, sliding the dildo up into her cunt and feeling for her clitoris with her index finger.

'Now, my dear,' continued the stallholder, 'place this bottle to your nose and breathe in the fragrance; the scented vapours will help to relax you whilst I insert the ring.'

He handed her a little green glass bottle which Madelon recognised instantly, for such aids were often used by the less experienced pupils at the Conservatoire, particularly when gaining their first clumsy experiences of anal intercourse. The vapours were both relaxing and stimulating, promoting a delightful sense of wellbeing and allowing comfortable penetration of even the tightest virgin arsehole.

Madelon remembered with amusement her own first experiences of anal penetration. Her cousin, Armand, had come to visit from Geneva, with tales of his sexual prowess and the many delights of life as a medical student at the university. Madelon was scarcely more than a child – a virgin only months before, and eagerly awaiting news of a vacancy at the Conservatoire. Armand told her that he would teach her some tricks which would stand her in good stead once she became a pupil . . .

One night, he had come to her room and hushed her cry of surprise with a kiss, pulling his nightshirt over his head and slipping quickly into bed beside her. She, being quite atrociously naive, had expected him to fuck her, or put his penis into her mouth so that she could suck him off. But to her surprise, he rolled her over on to her belly.

'What on earth are you doing, Armand?' she gasped, her face half buried in the pillow.

And he had told her how he had learned a new and delightful pleasure from the young boys who plied their trade among the university students. He was sure that she, too, would find it most agreeable.

Before she had a chance to question what he was doing, or protest in any way, Madelon felt Armand's strong hands opening her up, pulling apart her arse-cheeks; and a bold, shameless finger searching for her secret hole.

A thicker probe nudged its tip against her arse-hole, and without further ado, Armand had forced his penis deep into her arse. How she had howled with discomfort as his fat prick tore into her, for, medical student though he was, he had not thought to lubricate her, or to relax her with some subtle drug. How she wished she had had one of those little green bottles to ease her second passage into womanhood!

It was not until he buggered her a second time,

that same night, that Madelon had realised what a sublimely pleasurable experience it could be.

The peasant-girl inhaled the vapours from the bottle, and Madelon saw how her cunt became immediately wetter. The stallholder showed the girl's father how to massage his daughter's breasts and so both relax and excite her still further.

The spectators were all masturbating eagerly by now; and two middle-aged women had pulled open their bodices, and were toying with the rings which pierced each other's large, brown nipples.

The stallholder judged his moment precisely, and – just as the girl was ascending towards orgasm – he pushed the needle through her clitoris, swiftly following it with a tiny ring of the finest gold wire.

In spite of the soothing fragrance, the girl cried out with pain – but the stallholder was already on his knees between her thighs, his tongue toying with the ring. And almost immediately she forgot her pain, and Madelon saw the juices emerging from the girl's cunt and forming a wet trail down the inside of her thigh.

The peasant-girl came with a loud squeal of pleasure, her father testifying to the efficacy of the procedure by spurting his semen all over her exposed breasts. And the watching throng applauded in their own way, with torrents of spunk and cunt-juice.

Afterwards, much refreshed by her orgasm, Madelon handed back the dildo and continued on towards the restaurant.

She was about to sit down at one of the tables, when she felt a hand upon her shoulder.

'Madelon . . . ? Mademoiselle D'Abbeville?'

She turned to see the red and breathless face of a

young man, tall and blond and with a notebook and pen clutched in his hand.

'Yes. And you are . . . ?'

'Sidney Carter, of the *London Daily Globe*. I hope you'll pardon the intrusion, but they told me at the Conservatoire that I might find you here. I was rather hoping you might allow me to interview you, seeing as you're one of the finalists in the royal contest. May I buy you lunch? Perhaps then you could show me the sights of Friedenheim.'

Madelon smiled, and took pity on the young man in his confusion.

'Of course,' she said. 'Shall we sit here?' She indicated a curious little table in the shade of a large blue parasol. The table was made of a sheet of clear glass, and there was no tablecloth, so the diners could clearly observe each other from head to toe whilst they ate. The two chairs were also of a most original design, common throughout Friedenbourg but obviously quite new to Mr Carter, for he was staring at them in disbelief.

'The chair with the little spike sticking up out of it is for the lady,' explained Madelon, 'or for the gentleman who enjoys having his arse fucked. It is designed to fit snugly into either cunt or arse. The other chair is for the gentleman. It has a little harness which straps over your hips, and your penis slips into the leather sleeve. All my gentlemen friends tell me it is a most agreeable sensation, which produces a beautifully hard erection and powerful orgasm.'

'I'm afraid this is all very new to me,' replied Sidney, reddening with embarrassment. 'You'll have to show me what to do, Mademoiselle. I wouldn't want to offend any of your local customs.'

Madelon indicated that he should sit down, and he settled himself on his chair.

'Will you take out your penis, Mr Carter, or would you like me to do it for you?' she asked politely.

'I . . . please do, Mademoiselle. I'd be honoured.'

Gently but efficiently, Madelon unbuttoned Carter's trousers and reached inside for his penis. She always enjoyed that first moment of discovery. Would his prick be rampant and magnificent, or a flaccid disappointment?

She was pleased and relieved to find that Mr Carter possessed a very presentable penis: a little over the average length, and hard enough to satisfy any woman. It hardened still further at her delicate touch, and Carter gave a little sigh of pleasure as she stroked him prior to inserting his manhood into the leather sleeve.

Madelon adjusted the sleeve so that it fitted snugly about his shaft.

'All you have to do is move gently backwards and forwards,' explained Madelon. 'In that way, you can regulate your own orgasm.'

Sidney Carter was quite overwhelmed by the plethora of sensations which were flooding through his body. He took a furtive glance around the restaurant, and saw that most of the other diners were using similar chairs. One middle-aged and rather corpulent businessman was thrusting powerfully into a leather sheath whilst, kneeling on the floor between his feet, a young lad was licking his testicles.

Madelon saw what Sidney was looking at, and explained.

'For an extra few pfennigs, the serving-lads will lick your balls, or suck you off. Would you like me to call one over for you, Mr Carter?'

Carter stared at her, aghast.

'Oh, no . . . I mean, that's very kind of you, Mademoiselle, but my interests lie elsewhere.'

Madelon smiled. So it was true, then, that foreigners really did have narrow tastes and preferences, confining themselves only to liaisons with persons of the opposite sex. Amongst Friedenbourg's liberal citizens, no sexual activity was scorned if it gave pleasure – for the greatest pleasure of the greatest number was the philosophy by which the principality was governed.

Madelon determined to be hospitable. Perhaps she would succeed in converting him to her point of view. Besides which, she needed plenty of practice if she was going to do well in the forthcoming contest . . .

Pulling up her skirts to reveal the beauty of her creamy-white naked thighs and pubis, Madelon prepared to sit down upon her chair, positioning herself so that the wooden spike would slide smoothly and evenly up into her cunt. She pulled apart her cunt-lips, and Carter's eyes widened. There was no doubt at all that he could see the little gold clitty-ring, glittering among the folds of moist pink flesh.

She lowered herself on to the spike with a sigh of satisfaction, and called the waiter over to take their order. As Carter was staring fixedly at her cunt and thighs through the glass table-top, red-faced and dumbstruck, she ordered for him – a platter of cold meats and a stein of beer – and then turned back to him, intent on giving him the full benefit of her attention.

'Now, Mr Carter, what was it you wanted me to tell you about?'

'I . . . do you know, it's quite gone out of my mind.'

Carter writhed in delicious torment as the sheath seemed to tighten about his penis, and he felt compelled to thrust faster, harder, more powerfully still.

'Poor Mr Carter,' soothed Madelon, dipping the corner of her handkerchief into the fingerbowl, and mopping the beads of perspiration from his brow. 'The English must be a terribly repressed race – tell me, do they never even masturbate in public, or have public gardens for fucking?'

Carter laughed.

'My dear Mademoiselle Madelon,' he replied. 'In England, though our mighty Empire bestrides the world, in matters sexual we are but poor savages. Fucking is a private and almost shameful thing; and those who indulge in masturbation are vilified as degenerates. I cannot tell you how refreshing it is to come to this wonderful country, where all is open and . . . oh, my stars! I can feel it . . . ! Aah!'

His penis twitched convulsively, and a torrent of sperm gushed forth from the tip, spattering the underside of the table-top. Immediately, a waiter appeared as if from nowhere and wiped the table clean, then disappeared as quickly as he had come.

When Carter opened his eyes again, he saw that Madelon had finished eating and was busily masturbating herself. Gazing at her through the table-top, he saw how she manipulated the tiny gold ring, and how each successive caress made her clitty swell and her cunt drip juice, forming a light froth about the stalk of the surrogate penis.

As her orgasm approached, she began to raise herself from the chair and lower herself back down on to the wooden dildo, at first slowly and then increasingly faster, faster, faster . . . until at last, her pleasure came in long, loud gasps.

After they had finished their meal, Madelon took Sidney Carter on a tour of the city's many sights: the Palace of Congress, where Friedenheim's most beautiful and skilful professional whores acted out daily displays of their subtle art; the Aquarium, where couples fucked in a waist-deep pool surrounded by tropical fish, leaving little white trails of frothing sperm and cunt-juice in the blue-green waters; and finally, the Garden of Earthly Pleasures, where Friedenheim's citizens met to bestow and enjoy sexual delights.

They sat down on one of the marble benches, in the shade of a bank of exotic flowers and trees chosen for their oriental fragrances, breathing in the heady aphrodisiac aromas.

On the grass before them, citizens of all ages were fucking and gratifying their own and each other's bodies in every way imaginable. Carter's prick began to swell as he watched two young girls tumbling together on the warm sweet grass, their skirts above their waists, squealing with the pleasure that each other's lips and tongues were affording them.

Nearby, a group of adolescent boys and girls were being given an instructional talk and demonstration by two senior tutors from Friedenheim's Gymnasium, the local high school.

'They are being shown how to pleasure each other, in preparation for their first sexual experiences,' explained Madelon, as the two tutors set about fucking noisily upon the grass. 'It is considered a great misfortune for any citizen to remain a virgin after the age of seventeen; and those who have not enjoyed sexual intercourse by that age are fucked by a skilled tutor. Either that, or they are put into pairs and watched over as they enjoy their first fuck together. Either way, it is considered important that all adolescents should know the secrets of love and the basic skills of pleasure – for the body is a secret and sacred instrument, a delicate lute from which only a skilled player can strike a perfect note.

'Parents bring their children to the Gardens from an early age, so that they can see and marvel at the earthly delights which they, too, will one day enjoy.'

Carter had almost forgotten to keep taking notes, for his attention was quite severely distracted by the sight of a fearsome, leather-clad wench in a mask and spike-heeled boots. Though she was dressed in a mannish style, her flesh encased in tight leather breeches and jacket, the curves of her body were clearly visible through the skin-tight leather, and her breasts and cunt-lips protruded through slits in her clothes. She was cracking a bullwhip, whilst in her right hand she held the end of a long leather thong.

The other end of the thong was attached to a heavy silver ring; and the ring passed through the penis of a rather distinguished but entirely naked middle-aged man, who was following her placidly through the gardens like a dog on a leash. As though to reinforce this effect, he wore a spiked leather dog-collar around his throat.

'That is the Mayor of Friedenheim,' said Madelon, in answer to Carter's questioning look. 'He has a very fine penis, does he not?'

At that moment, a dark-haired young man in top hat and white gloves approached, and bowed low before Madelon.

'Excuse me, my dear sir,' he addressed Carter.

'But I am most desirous of fucking your lady companion. May I have the honour?'

Carter glanced at Madelon, who smiled and nodded, and he replied:

'I . . . yes, certainly.'

The young blade proceeded to unfasten his flies and take out a good-sized, well-formed penis. Its purple head glistened against the dazzling white of his fine calfskin gloves, and Madelon felt an agreeable wave of desire wash over her.

He presented his prick to her like some priceless gift, and Madelon bent her head forward to kiss it with all due reverence. It tasted both salty and sweet, and carried with it the heady aroma of exotic unguents, used by many of the wealthy citizens to increase their potency and prolong pleasure.

She took the engorged stalk into her mouth, and teased it, running her tongue around the tip as though tasting some rare and delicious sweetmeat. And she slipped her hands through the young man's open flies and pulled out his twin fruits, sapengorged and ripe for the bursting.

To her surprise, he pulled back before she had brought him to orgasm, and pushed her gently back against the wrought-iron bench. He knelt down on the warm grass and felt among the rustling silk for the hem of her gown. Finding it at last, he pulled up her skirts until they were round her waist, and bent to kiss her intimacy. He parted her cunt-lips with gentle gloved fingers, and his delighted tongue began to toy with the fine gold clitty-ring.

She sighed with pleasure as he brought her to orgasm – once, twice, again . . . And then fell upon her with a joyful cry, his penis thrusting into her warm wetness again and again, until at last they lay together, exhausted, on the bench in the warm sunshine.

Afterwards, the young man saluted her with a respectful kiss on the hand, then turned to Sidney.

'Your lady friend is a most pleasing fuck, my good man. Never before have I felt such a silken tongue, such wetness about my prick, and yet such tightness also! You are a lucky man, Herr . . . ?'

'Carter, Sidney Carter . . . of the *London Daily Globe*.'

The young man bowed once again, picked up his top hat and, brushing off a little stray blossom, placed it back on his head. 'I bid you a good day, Herr Carter and Fräulein . . . ?'

'Just call me Madelon.'

And he was gone.

'Who on earth was that?' asked Sidney, trying to compose himself and quieten down the dreadfully troublesome erection which was bulging the front of his trousers with quite obscene insistence.

Madelon shook her head, not quite sure and yet wondering . . . Could it really have been . . . ?

'I'm sorry, I don't know,' she replied.

But at the back of her mind, she couldn't help wondering if her transitory suitor really could have been Prince Albrecht von Friedenbourg.

Chasing the thought from her mind, Madelon turned to Sidney Carter with an engaging smile.

'I've shown you the sights of the city,' she said. 'Now it's your turn, Mr Carter. You tell me you're staying at the Hotel Neusteiner? I understand they have extremely comfortable beds.'

45

3   The Contest

Madelon reached out for the clock, and realised with horror that it was almost six o'clock in the morning. She had slept the whole night through! If she didn't hurry, she would be late for the ceremonial robing at Castle Amor.

She tried to creep out of bed without disturbing Sidney, but his arm was still across her naked body. As she lifted it to free herself, he awoke and pulled her to him, dragging her nakedness back into the bed and close to his groin. His penis was hard and pulsating against the flesh of her backside.

'I must go, Sidney. I didn't sign out last night – you know we're supposed to tell Matron if we're spending the night with a man – and if I don't hurry, I'm going to miss being presented to the Prince!'

Sidney laughed, and stroked Madelon's breast with playful fingers.

'Surely you've got time for . . . once more?'

'No, no, really I haven't!' Madelon found herself giggling as Sidney ran his fingertips down her belly and foraged in the fragrant depths of her pubic hair.

She knew her willpower had deserted her.

Wriggling round in the bed, she turned to face her English lover. He meant nothing to her, and soon she would have forgotten him – and yet he had learnt so much since they had met, only hours before. He was an apt pupil. It would be a shame not to complete his sexual education . . .

She slid down underneath the bedclothes, and fastened her greedy lips around the journalist's engorged penis. It tasted strong and salty, still coated with dried semen and cunt-juices. He groaned – a long sigh of utter pleasure – as she slid her hand between his thighs, pressing upwards against his testicles.

She sucked at him and massaged his balls, feeling her own desire mounting with his, feeling the throbbing in her clitoris becoming a raging, burning furnace as his spunk jetted out into her willing mouth, and she swallowed it down, every drop. Sweeter than nectar.

He was thrusting her legs apart now, and searching for her clitty-ring with his tongue. Oh, the ecstasy as he found it and began to turn it slowly between tongue and teeth, skilfully finding just the right hairsbreadth moment between agony and ecstasy; until at last he made her come, oozing slippery cunt-juice as though it were welling up from some eternal spring.

When he had rested for a little while, she masturbated him back to rigidity and straddled him, riding him bareback until they exploded together in a torrent of mutual joy.

Afterwards, when they had dozed in each other's arms for a few moments, Madelon pushed back the covers and slid quietly out of bed.

'Now I really must go,' she whispered, planting a kiss on his closed eyelids.

Madelon, Alex and Florence waited with the other

candidates in the anteroom to the Grand Hall at Castle Amor. The atmosphere was one of extreme tension. Outside the castle walls, crowds of citizens were waiting: waiting to see who would be the winner of the contest, and the future Crown Princess of Friedenbourg.

The eight girls had arrived at the Castle at dawn, and were received by Frau Agathe, Prince Albrecht's governess and tutor in all matters sexual. She had prepared each girl individually, bathing her and dressing her in a richly embroidered robe. It was considered most important that, however rich or poor the girls might be, there should be no obvious divisions of class or wealth to hamper their chances in the contest.

And so it was that a peasant, an Indian princess, a gypsy, a ballerina, a trapeze artist and three pupils from the Conservatoire waited together in the anteroom, trying not to be nervous and casting critical glances at the other candidates. Who was the most beautiful? More important, who would turn out to be the most sensually gifted? And which of them would succeed in gratifying the Prince?

Florence gritted her teeth in determination, and mentally ran through all the different stimulation techniques she had mastered in the last few weeks. Others might have been surprised at her meteoric success in the preliminary rounds of the contest, but it came as no surprise to Florence. She was going to succeed. She knew in her heart that she was by far the most naturally gifted of all the candidates, and she was going to be the next Crown Princess of Friedenbourg.

By her side, Alex sat in abject terror, wondering why she had ever allowed her name to be put forward, and what dreadful twist of fate had decreed that she should be chosen as one of the eight finalists. She recalled her preliminary audition, in which she had – to her own amazement – succeeded in sucking off four of the Prince's envoys in rapid succession. It was all a mystery to her, really: normally she was just hopeless at oral sex. Her technique was never quite right – too hard with the teeth, or not thorough enough with the tongue . . . but on that fateful day, a week ago, she had been among the finest fellatrices in the land.

Madelon glanced around the room, and wondered if all of this was really true. Was she really good enough to be considered as a future bride for the Crown Prince? Her clitoris throbbed, reminding her of all the men – and women – she had fucked over the last couple of days, in preparation for the day's ordeals. By a tremendous act of will, she refrained from slipping her hand through the folds of her robe and masturbating herself.

She must save herself for the contest.

'The Prince is ready. Bring in the candidates.'

As Frau Agathe finished speaking, double doors opened at the far end of the anteroom, and two footmen in full royal livery ushered the girls into the Grand Hall.

Madelon gasped in amazement at the opulence around her. The walls were richly painted with frescoes depicting erotic scenes from mythology, and as she looked down at her feet she saw that she was walking across a mosaic formed entirely from precious and semi-precious stones, beautifully shaped to form a picture of two satyrs fucking and buggering a naked wood-nymph. Even each crystal droplet in the massive chandeliers was shaped like a tiny penis or a miniature breast.

Prince Albrecht sat on a small, jewelled throne at the far end of the Hall, unable to occupy the royal throne of Friedenbourg because he was as yet uncrowned. First, he must find himself a wife.

Madelon hardly dared look at him. But she recognised him instantly, though he looked very different in his ornate robes of state. The tall young man who had fucked her so graciously in the park . . . the dark-haired aristocrat with the white gloves and delightfully firm penis – that had been Prince Albrecht. She had already fucked Prince Albrecht!

She felt sure that he must have recognised her instantly, too; and wondered if this meant that she would be disqualified from the contest. She couldn't look him in the eye.

'Your Royal Highness,' announced Frau Agathe, 'I have brought before you the eight young ladies chosen by myself and your advisers as the most agreeable and suited to the high office of Crown Princess. Each has passed a preliminary examination of skill and beauty, and I now bring them before you for your inspection and to undergo additional trials of skill and endurance.'

Prince Albrecht nodded – somewhat wearily, thought Madelon. Could it be that he found none of them agreeable?

Madelon cast a sidelong glance at the Prince, and could not suppress a little shiver of anticipation, for he was every bit as handsome as she remembered. He wore a long, ermine-trimmed cloak, embroidered with the figures of unicorns with massively erect penises, delicately worked in the finest gold thread.

Beneath the cloak, he was all but naked. His fine

penis – erect already, for he had drunk a powerful infusion of aphrodisiac herbs in preparation for the ceremony – was encased in a silken sheath, which was attached to his balls by means of a gold harness. Madelon found herself longing to slide that beautiful cock out of its sheath, and find it a far better hiding-place, in the moist darkness of her mouth.

'Bring the young ladies before me, each in turn,' commanded the Prince. 'I wish to give them a more intimate examination.'

Frau Agathe ushered the first girl forward: a sloe-eyed beauty with olive skin and the grace of a dancer.

'What is your name, child?' the Prince demanded. 'Tell me a little about yourself.'

'My name is Isabella, your Highness,' she replied. 'And I am a dancer at the Theatre of Nubile Beauty. I came to Friedenbourg two years ago, as a ballerina, because I wanted more scope to display my body.'

'Take off your robe. I wish to examine your nakedness.'

The girl obeyed, untying her sash and slipping the robe down over her shoulders, so that it fell in multicoloured, gauzy folds about her naked feet. She stepped out of it daintily, and walked gracefully towards the Prince, kneeling in all her comely nakedness before him.

He stooped, and ran his practised hand over the budding flesh of her nipples, two perfect rosebuds on the tiny mounds of her breasts. Her flesh became taut at his touch, and her breath quickened.

'You respond well, my dear,' nodded the Prince. 'Though your breasts are rather small for my tastes. Stand up, girl, and let me explore your delightful body a little more closely.'

She stood before him, and he slid his hand down her flank and over the smooth flesh of her buttocks, giving little grunts of approval. His fingers grew bolder, and delved into the dark triangle of her pubic hair.

'You have a nice, tight hole, Isabella,' remarked the Prince, approvingly. 'And have undoubtedly given great pleasure to many men.'

He dismissed her with a kiss upon each nipple, and she slipped her robe back on, going back to sit with the others.

The next candidate to be presented was the precocious Florence, all blue eyes and long blonde hair, now untied from its restricting plaits and allowed to cascade in endless golden ringlets over her shoulders, like a golden waterfall. Her breasts were youthful and not yet quite fully developed, but they were fuller than Isabella's and the nipples were long and firm, like betel nuts begging to be bitten.

She fluttered her eyelids at the Prince, and when his hand touched her, she thrust out her breasts, encouraging him to appreciate their firmness and feel their weight.

He murmured appreciatively as he judged the almost virgin tightness of Florence's cunt, no doubt wondering what it would feel like to bury his prick inside her. But the silly girl made the mistake of letting her confidence overcome her good sense.

'I should dearly love to suck you off, your Highness,' she announced as he fingered her wet crack.

She could not have done a worse thing than speak to the Prince when she had not first been addressed by him. Immediately a cloud passed across his face and he sent her back to her seat without a further word.

The dark-eyed, scarlet-lipped gypsy Elena knew that she was a match for any Prince. A pure-bred Romany princess, and the seventh daughter of a seventh daughter, she had bewitched the Prince's emissaries when they happened upon her in the forests near Castle Amor, dancing naked on the moonlit grass amid a circle of delighted admirers.

She bent her head respectfully, all the time making sure that the Prince had a good view of the deep cleavage between her succulent breasts.

'Take off your robe, and approach the throne.'

She let the jewelled fabric slip from her shoulders, so slowly and seductively that it seemed the whole world held its breath, waiting for the divine revelation of her wonderful body.

She was nut-brown and her skin glowed with health, her nipples a darker brown against the tanned flesh of her breasts. She looked up at the Prince, and he felt her fire entering him, consuming him alive. She was bewitching him; he knew it, and yet he could not resist. He did not want to resist. He wanted only to sink in her arms, to feel her thighs slipping apart to let him into her soft, wet cunt. His hand slid between her thighs, and he shivered with delight as the heat radiated from her and the fragrant juices dripped on to his fingers.

He had to fuck her. He had to . . .

At that moment, a side-door opened, and a messenger scurried in, bowing low before the Prince and no doubt greatly fearing his wrath.

'Your Royal Highness, pray forgive me,' he stuttered. 'But a matter of grave importance . . .'

'You may continue,' said the Prince, calmly.

'A man from the gypsy camp is here. He claims that the woman Elena is his wife!'

The spell was broken. The Prince looked back at Elena and saw that she was scowling with resentment.

'Son of a pig!' she cried. 'That *batardo* Rodolphe – it was to be our secret . . . but he would not keep his side of the bargain, no! I will kill him!' And, in the absence of the unwilling accomplice Rodolphe, she fetched the poor messenger a terrific swipe across the face, making his knees buckle.

The Prince watched in amusement as the gypsy-girl raged before him, a parody of her former seductive self.

'My dear Elena,' he sighed. 'Since you are already married, you cannot become my wife. But you may, in time, become one of my favoured mistresses . . .'

But Elena merely scowled at the Prince and, to his utter amazement, threw the jewelled robe in his face before flouncing out of the Grand Hall, slamming the door behind her.

The sound echoed around the chamber for many moments before, at last, Frau Agathe cleared her throat and introduced the next girl to the Prince.

'The Princess Shireen, your Royal Highness.'

The Indian princess was tall, slender and elegant, and the Prince smiled with satisfaction as she took off her robe, revealing two perfect diamond drops, hanging on silver chains from her pierced nipples. As she parted her legs for his inspection, he saw with pleasure that her outer cunt-lips were also pierced with diamond studs, and linked by another long, silver chain which hung enticingly between her thighs. Her dark brown eyes sparkled with secret knowledge, and the Prince sent her back to her seat with an encouraging smile.

Next came Alex – whose robust English frame and

perfect peaches-and-cream complexion seemed to please the Prince. He even seemed to find delight in her innocent inexperience. She was followed by Hilde, the local favourite: a sturdy blonde peasant-girl with huge breasts and a delightfully open disposition. Brought up in the ways of Friedenbourg, she took a peasant's simple delight in fucking, and the Prince stroked her generous breasts with obvious pleasure.

Nancy was an American acrobat – a trapeze-artist and gymnast from Chicago who had come to Friedenheim with a travelling circus and had been so delighted with the local customs that she had decided to stay and join the city's resident troupe. The Friedenbourg circus was not quite like its traditional counterpart for, like everything in the principality, it had a strong sexual element. Nancy's prowess in sexual gymnastics was renowned throughout the city, and no doubt the Prince thought back to some of the charming evenings he and his father had spent at the circus, watching her perform by royal command.

At last it was Madelon's turn. She froze at the command from Frau Agathe to go forward, momentarily paralysed with fear. Why had she got involved in the contest? Did she really want to marry the Prince anyway? Her mind was a whirling confusion of anxieties.

'Don't be afraid: I won't bite you!'

The Prince's voice jolted her back to reality, and she took a few steps forward, still trembling underneath the richly embroidered robe. She must try to remember what she had been taught. A pupil of the Conservatoire must promote the pleasure of others

55

at all times. She must submit herself to their joy, utterly and without question.

She slipped off the robe and ascended the steps to the dais on which the Prince was sitting, kneeling before him, head bowed, half in respect, half in terror.

'I remember you, my dear Mademoiselle,' whispered the Prince, as he bent to stroke her breasts. 'The adorable little Swiss girl with the pierced clitty. I think I should like to make its acquaintance again soon. Very soon . . .'

As she stood before him, legs parted, he explored first her arse – verifying that it was sufficiently tight to give pleasure – and then the moist, pink folds of her cunt. He thrust his finger into her cunt and gave her clitty ring a little tug; and she almost died of mingled pain and pleasure.

When he sent her back to her seat, he looked well pleased.

The three finalists were announced later that morning. They were Nancy, Hilde and Madelon. Florence stormed back to the Conservatoire in tears, and spent the rest of the day lying on her bed, wondering how she could take her revenge on those who had stolen her rightful prize from her.

The final judging of the contest was to take place that night, at the Castle, in front of twenty of the Prince's most senior advisers. In order to claim her reward and marry the Prince, the winner must perform feats of 'sexual delight and ingenuity' which would charm the hearts and pricks of those watching.

The programme began with Hilde, the local peasant-girl, whom everyone was expecting to win comfortably. She entered the Hall, dressed in her usual peasant clothing and carrying a little wooden bowl. She carried it across to where the Prince's Chancellor was sitting, and placed it between his feet. Then she reached up and unfastened his trousers, taking out his well-stiffened prick.

'Milking time,' she breathed, gripping his prick firmly and beginning to masturbate it, at first gently, but then with increasing fervour.

'Charming, charming girl . . . !' gasped the Chancellor, clutching at Hilde's blonde hair as she wanked him off. 'Such a deliciously firm touch . . .'

The old man spurted out his semen, and Hilde collected it in her bowl. She moved around the room, from one dignitary to another, at each point collecting the semen in her little wooden bowl, until at last it was brimming with the white, frothy liquid.

She walked towards the Prince, laid the bowl at his feet, and began to unfasten her bodice.

In years to come, all Friedenbourg still talked of the night when the pretty farm-girl, Hilde, had rubbed her breasts with semen and then massaged still more of the opalescent fluid into the Prince's prick and balls. They told of how she licked off every drop of the cold semen from his prick; of how she had whipped herself with a bunch of fresh birch-twigs and then turned the weapon upon the Prince himself, defying his royal birth to turn him from prince into victim.

How the Prince cried out as the twigs dealt him a stinging blow across the base of his penis, and a torrent of answering spunk gushed forth from its tip.

Nancy, the circus performer, delighted her audience with a display of agile sex, the like of which they had never seen before in their lives. She performed for them on a high-wire, slung across the

Hall from one side to the other, ten feet off the ground; and she masturbated for them as she straddled the wire. Then, with an agile flip, she sprang backwards, landing on feet and hands so that her body was splayed out, crab-fashion. She then invited the Prince to join her in this unholy congress, and he fucked her with great energy – two beasts rutting together in the primeval forest.

At last it was Madelon's turn. To give herself courage, she had donned a black mask, hoping that it would render her more mysterious. Across her shoulders lay a black leather cape, but other than that she was naked. She carried a cat-o'-nine-tails, the thongs made from soft, pliable leather but tipped with cruel lead-shot.

She prostrated herself before the Prince, and handed him the cat. Silently imploring him to whip her, she lay before him, bare-fleshed and helpless, and he did as she wished him to, reddening the flesh of her back, buttocks and thighs with repeated strokes of the lash.

When he tired, she took the lash from him and whipped her own flesh, playing its wicked tip across the softness of her belly and breasts, until they too were reddened and covered in raised welts.

To the Prince's surprise, Madelon suddenly turned upon him, ripping off his robe and exposing the nakedness beneath. In a frenzy of savagery, she brought the lash down on his back and buttocks; then turned the cat the other way round and – lubricating the plaited leather handle with her own spittle and cunt-juice – she insinuated its tip between the Prince's buttocks.

How he writhed as the tip entered his flesh, buried itself deep within him. Madelon did not stop until almost the whole of the handle was inside him, with only the very tip protruding from his arsehole.

Then she turned her back on him, propped herself up on the arms of the throne, and offered her own backside to the Prince. Fortified with powerful aphrodisiac herbs, he was ready for her, and thrust his stiff prick between her arse-cheeks with a cry of joy.

The little love-eggs inside Madelon's cunt rubbed deliciously together, and stimulated the Prince's prick through the fragile wall of her arse, giving him the most exquisite pleasure. She squeezed her cunt-walls tight, so that the pressure on his penis became even greater, even more delightful; and then she reached backwards, one hand between her parted thighs, and toyed with the Prince's twin fruits, gently squeezing them in her palm.

The joy of orgasm overcame her suddenly, and as her cunt twitched in ecstasy, the Prince shot his load into her arse.

Afterwards, the Prince and his ministers retired to the anteroom to discuss the candidates. The final outcome was uncertain. Would he choose Nancy, the bold, ingenious acrobat? Or Madelon, the masked temptress with the arse like burning velvet? Or Hilde, the buxom beauty, wise in country lore?

At last, the announcement was made. The Chancellor stepped forward and spoke to the assembled courtiers:

'My lords and ladies; the selection has been difficult – so difficult that the Prince has been quite unable to choose an outright winner. He is undecided between Hilde and Madelon, who in his eyes have been seen to have precisely equal merits.'

The Hall was in an uproar. A tie! But this was

quite impossible – the Prince could not have more than one Princess! What was he to do?

'And so,' continued the Chancellor, 'it has been decided that the outcome of the contest shall be determined by the candidates themselves. Madelon and Hilde shall meet in sexual combat, the winner to marry the Prince and be crowned Princess of Friedenbourg. The contest will take place this evening, in the castle gardens, and will continue until one of the candidates submits to the other.'

The Chancellor's speech caused a sensation. As the candidates were dismissed, to rest for the rest of the day, courtiers and ministers talked animatedly about constitutional crises, legal precedents and state protocol. Never had such a thing happened before.

Madelon was in confusion. What did all of this mean? She hurried back to the Conservatoire, she mused over what she would have to do that evening.

As she walked towards the room which she shared with Alex, she passed the open door of the dormitory in which the junior girls slept. She glanced inside, and was just in time to see Florence Desfarges glaring at her. If looks could kill . . .

When she reached her room, she was greeted eagerly by Alex, who was extremely pleased to have been chosen as a finalist, but even more relieved not to be in Madelon's position. Alex was full of eager congratulation.

'Oh Madelon – you have done so well! It's such a shame the Prince didn't choose you straight away – none of the other girls were a patch on you!'

Madelon took off her dress and lay down on the bed, her comely nakedness warmed and enhanced by the rays of the afternoon sun which filtered through the half-closed shutters. 'Oh Alex, I'm just pleased to have got this far,' she sighed, stretching cat-like on the warm counterpane.

Alex climbed on the bed and lay on her side, gently stroking Madelon's creamy-white flesh. Her fingers soothed and teased and aroused, all at once.

'You must rest, Madelon,' she breathed. 'Let me help you to relax.'

And her fingers wandered down Madelon's belly, stroking the flesh, finely toned and yet soft and sensual. She explored Madelon's golden pubic fleece, twining the curls around her fingers and then letting them dive and delve further in, into Madelon's innermost intimacy.

'Ah . . .' sighed Madelon, parting her thighs to allow Alex's fingers to continue their exploration. Alex was exploring her cunt now, and discovering to her delight that it was hot and wet and ready for her.

And now she was scooping up the juices from her cunt and spreading them over her clitoris, moistening it for her gentle touch. Stroking, stroking, rubbing so gently . . . it felt like a butterfly's kiss, again and again and again.

And, with a long sigh of pleasure, Madelon came to an orgasm that was long and sweet and luxurious.

Afterwards, she curled up in Alex's arms, and drifted off into a dreamless slumber.

4   The Decision

The Chancellor signalled to the Prince that the two candidates were ready, and the Prince nodded.

'Let the contest begin.'

The Prince's throne had been carried out into the gardens of Castle Amor, which at this time of year were a riot of colours and scents. As was the custom in Friedenbourg, the gardens had been filled with a variety of plants chosen for their aphrodisiac qualities; and these had been enhanced by the inclusion of erotic statues sculpted by the principality's finest artists and craftsmen.

The contest was to take place in a grassy glade amidst fragrant jasmine and oleanders, the gathering dusk illuminated by dozens of lamps, hanging from the trees like exotic glow-worms. Amongst the trees sat the Prince's ten most senior advisers, who would judge that the contest was proceeding fairly and pronounce upon its outcome.

Hilde and Madelon advanced towards the middle of the clearing, where they embraced each other, as ceremony demanded.

As they bent to kiss each other's throats, Madelon heard Hilde whisper in her ear:

'Don't think for a moment that you're going to win, you stuck-up little cow. You can try and try, but I'm going to make you submit to me. I'm going to give you the orgasm of your life . . . and I'm going to be the next Crown Princess of Friedenbourg.'

Madelon stepped back, visibly shaken by what her opponent had said. There was a steely glint in Hilde's eye, and Madelon suddenly began to feel exceedingly nervous. Maybe she shouldn't have agreed to take part in the contest. Madelon wasn't even from Friedenbourg, and Hilde was the local favourite, after all. Perhaps Madelon ought to give in and proclaim her the victor?

But a tide of anger was rising in her, despite her fears. Why should she give up her own claim, just because Hilde was trying to intimidate her? And she had a feeling that Hilde was going to try and cheat in some way – her right fist was tightly clenched, as though she were trying to conceal something within it. Madelon despised cheats and frauds.

And it was too late to change her mind now. The two girls, clad only in short, gold-belted diaphanous tunics, were already facing each other, like two Roman gladiators, each wary of making the first move.

Madelon took the initiative, stretching out her hand and stroking Hilde's massive right breast through the gauzy fabric. The nipple stiffened a little, but Hilde's face betrayed no sign of emotion or arousal.

Hilde reached out and, in one swift movement, tore down the front of Madelon's tunic, exposing her pink-nippled breasts. The suddenness of the assault, the fragrance in the air, the coolness of the night-breeze on her breasts . . . all conspired to make Madelon gasp with unexpected pleasure. Hilde was grinning now, and out of the corner of her eye

Madelon saw the judges writing something down – they were obviously awarding Hilde the advantage.

Madelon tried to retaliate, but Hilde was too quick for her. Before Madelon realised what was happening, Hilde had put her strong arms around her and was kissing her – ferociously, without gentleness. Her rose-scented breath entered Madelon like some narcotic draught, weakening her resistance still further.

She must not submit to Hilde's sexual tyranny. She must not respond to her crushing lips, her thrusting tongue, the boldness of her fingers . . .

And yet she could not help it.

Hilde's hands were all over her now; it felt as though she were being stroked and pinched by a dozen pairs of hands, not one. Hilde was a skilful lover, and she knew it. Desperately, Madelon reached out and managed to get hold of one of Hilde's nipples, which she succeeded in taking into her mouth. Hilde gave a stifled groan of mingled pleasure and indignation as Madelon began to tease the nipple with her tongue and teeth. The judges began scribbling again.

Point two: this time, in Madelon's favour.

But Madelon was losing badly. Hilde had succeeded in ripping off her tunic almost entirely, and its last torn vestiges were hanging in shreds from her golden belt. Her flesh was covered in tiny beads of sweat, and a slow trickle was disappearing between her breasts. Hilde's arms were still around her, and now she was lifting her – her feet were leaving the ground, kicking out wildly, but it was no use. Hilde was too strong for her.

Crushed against Hilde's mighty breasts, Madelon felt tiny and vulnerable – a little baby, fighting for its mother's milk. She managed to find Hilde's nipple and took it into her mouth again, sucking and biting as hard as she could. And she felt Hilde's heart-beat quickening, her breathing becoming more laboured as she fought to control the sensations of lust which were insinuating themselves into her disobedient body.

Hilde succeeded in wresting her nipple from Madelon's mouth, and laid down her opponent's body, pinning her to the ground. Even the moist coolness of the grass seemed sensual now. She clenched her teeth and tried not to groan as Hilde tried to prise her legs apart. If she succeeded, Madelon would surely be forced to submit. The thought of Hilde's lips and tongue and fingers, tormenting her gold clitty-ring, filled her mind with such a terrible vision of desire that Madelon knew she must soon be lost utterly.

Hilde's hand was between Madelon's thighs, and her fingers were creeping ever-closer to the golden clitty-ring. Her hand uncurled, and Madelon knew what Hilde had been concealing from her – a tiny dildo, which she would surely force up inside Madelon's cunt and make her come. Already Madelon could feel the juices welling up inside her, ready to pour forth uncontrollably. Her clitoris throbbed in unruly anticipation, longing for the touch or the kiss to which it knew it must not respond . . .

But fortune smiled on Madelon, and anger made her strong: for she suddenly realised that Hilde was forced to balance on one hand in order to lie above her, pinning her to the ground and probing between her thighs with the other hand. If she could be distracted in some way, perhaps Madelon could make her overbalance . . . ?

She managed to get one hand free, and with it, guided one of Hilde's pendulous breasts to her mouth. The touch of her tongue and teeth had an almost electric effect on Hilde, making her convulse with silent and unwilling pleasure. At last, her hand ceased its terrible exploration between Madelon's thighs.

Relentless in her determination, Madelon continued to suck at Hilde's breast, and she felt the peasant-girl weakening. Seizing her moment, she threw all her weight against Hilde's left arm, and almost cried out with the joy of success as the elbow gave way, and Hilde toppled sideways on to the grass.

Quick as a flash, Madelon was upon her. Hilde had the advantage of weight and strength, but Madelon was agile and skilful; and she gave her opponent no quarter. Try as she might, Hilde could find no opportunity to break free and get to her feet.

Whilst Hilde was still dazed with pleasure and confused by Madelon's sudden move, Madelon prised her thighs apart and exposed the treasures of her womanhood: a moist, pink pearl in a fine, fur-trimmed casket.

Hilde sensed her defeat approaching, but was too drunk with pleasure to resist. The little dildo fell from her grasp on to the grass. The judges saw it and the Lord Chancellor glanced towards Albrecht as though asking him to intervene, but the Prince shook his head.

'Do not disqualify the girl,' he said. 'Let us see what Madelon makes of the advantage that fortune has given her. Young Madelon now has the upper hand, and it is for Madelon herself to mete out justice.'

It was poetic justice indeed. For Madelon seized the dildo and, before Hilde could resist, thrust it home into the peasant-girl's cunt. Hilde gave a muffled cry of pleasure as Madelon worked the dildo in and out of her cunt, and bent to place her lips upon the secret treasure of Hilde's clitoris.

Hilde came with a loud shriek of ecstasy, and lay panting and half-dazed on the cool, damp grass.

When Madelon looked up from her labours, she saw the Prince standing over her, and she immediately bowed her head respectfully.

The Prince laughed.

'My dear Madelon,' he said. 'There is no need to cower so before me. You did not cower the first time we met – do you remember? You were such a delicious fuck, and I so hoped we would meet and fuck again. And now you are to be my wife – the new Crown Princess of Friedenbourg!'

Madelon accepted his proffered hand and rose rather unsteadily to her feet. Hilde was still lying on the ground, the dildo protruding from her cunt and a little pool of cunt-juice glistening on the dark grass.

It all seemed so unreal. And for the first time, Madelon paused to ask herself if she really wanted to marry Albrecht, Crown Prince of Friedenbourg.

The next morning, Madelon awoke not in her own room, but in her own private apartments in Castle Amor. Instead of her tiny shared room at the Conservatoire, she had her own bedroom with an enormous four-poster bed, her own sitting room, and an army of maids and footmen to attend to her needs. She had even been given a maid and footman charged with looking after her sexual needs at any hour of the day or night. But the first thing she did as soon as she was settled in her apartments was ask if her dear friend Alex might join her, as her lady-in-waiting.

Much relieved that she was going to be Madelon's lady-in-waiting, and not the Crown Princess, Alex arrived at Castle Amor around lunchtime. Madelon was quite beautifully naked, and was ushering yet another journalist into her private chamber. Thinking she might have chosen a bad moment, Alex turned to go, but Madelon beckoned her inside.

'No, please don't go, Alex. You can help with this interview: it shall be your very first duty as my lady-in-waiting!'

This particular journalist was from one of the most prestigious French newspapers, which was proposing to issue an illustrated supplement to commemorate the royal wedding and the contest which had enabled Prince Albrecht to select a suitable bride. He had brought a photographer with him, and they were busily discussing suitable poses for Madelon to adopt.

'Could you show us, please, how exactly you succeeded in finally overcoming your opponent?'

Madelon was more than happy to oblige – but who should play the part of Hilde? She beckoned to Alex: 'Alex, dear, would you mind terribly taking off your clothes just for a little while? These gentlemen would like to take a picture recording the moment when Hilde submitted to me.'

Alex slipped off her uniform blouse and skirt, and Madelon saw to her satisfaction that she was naked underneath. She had rather suspected that, once she was no longer at the Conservatoire to keep an eye on her dearest friend, Alex might slip back into her old ways. Oh, the difficulty the Headmistress had had in persuading Alex to abandon her sensible English knickers, and the dreary camisole top she had been wearing when she arrived! The poor girl had taken such a long time to understand the special pleasures of nakedness.

Madelon embraced Alex with such fervour that the poor girl was quite startled, but felt her clitty swelling with pleasure and pride. Madelon showed her where to lie and exactly how to arrange her limbs.

'That's right, Alex – slightly on your side, with your thighs very wide apart, so that the gentlemen can see what a pretty pussy you have. And then I shall put the dildo into you – there! Does that feel comfortable? May I kiss your clitty now, so that the gentlemen can take their photographs?'

Alex murmured her almost unintelligible assent, struck dumb with pleasure as Madelon's lips brushed her clitoris. The photographer lit the flash-powder, and the scene was immortalised for the paper's august readers.

'Just once more, ladies, if you please – that's beautiful. Exquisite! Hold it there . . .'

Another bright flash, and all was done.

The photographer and journalist packed their equipment away and were about to go when Madelon smiled and said, most apologetically, 'Oh, gentlemen – I've been so inhospitable! Won't you stay a while longer, and enjoy a little of our hospitality?'

Seeing the looks of incomprehension on their faces, Madelon explained:

'As you know, we in Friedenbourg have many

quaint customs which may seem strange to you. They were strange to me, too, when first I came to the Conservatoire. But I soon learned that the chief duty and concern of all citizens is to promote the pleasure of others. We live for pleasure, Messieurs, and will never deny it to anyone.'

'I . . . do not quite understand, Madame,' exclaimed the journalist, though his stiffening prick told a quite different story.

'My dear Monsieur,' intervened Alex. 'Mademoiselle Madelon and I are anxious only to serve your utmost pleasure. Let us offer ourselves to you for your delight. As you have seen, we have fine tight cunts, and am sure your pricks will not be disappointed with our welcome.'

Madelon was already on her knees in front of the photographer, unfastening the buttons of his trousers, and reaching inside for his prick, which sprang out with enthusiasm at her skilful touch.

Realising that these luscious young women were indeed serious in their offer, the journalist turned to Alex and began to massage her breast with a slow, circular motion, gradually pushing her, little by little, towards the four-poster bed.

Madelon was sucking the photographer's penis, teasing it into erection, and he was shaking his head and crying out:

'No, no – *pour l'amour de Dieu* – let me fuck you, Mademoiselle! *Que vous m'ouvriez votre divin con* . . . let me inside your heavenly cunt, my dear Mademoiselle!'

And Madelon and Alex fucked their guests side by side on the four-poster bed. If Prince Maximilian von Frieden was looking down on her, he would undoubtedly have been more than pleased with his future daughter-in-law.

Five hundred miles away, in a garret in Heidelberg, a young man in a tattered black suit was reading a newspaper. He was a tall young man, broad-shouldered and with flashing blue eyes; and he seemed out of place amid such poverty.

On the table lay a few stale crusts of bread and half a pitcher of sour red wine. The few sticks of furniture were rickety and worm-eaten.

The young man turned the page of the newspaper and gasped as he saw the photograph. Madelon and Prince Albrecht smiled out at him from the page, and the headline proclaimed the news of their forth-coming wedding.

But it was not the blushing bride-to-be who captured this reader's attention. He was staring fixedly at the picture of Prince Albrecht, as though coming to terms with some momentous and unacceptable realisation.

Then he got up from the table and went over to the wall, where an old cracked mirror hung, slightly askew on the dingy brown wallpaper. He stared at his reflection for a long time, deep in thought.

The carriage drew up outside the Conservatoire, and two figures got out: distinguished gentlemen of perhaps forty-five, no older, with just a touch of grey to add distinction at the temples.

Frau Kässler welcomed them into her study with cries of recognition.

'Monsieur D'Abbeville, how pleased I am to see you again. Is the news not wonderful?'

Madelon's father kissed Frau Kässler's ringed hand and smiled.

'My dear Frau Kässler, Madelon could never have aspired to such heights without your expert guidance and tuition. Now, if you will allow me to introduce to you Monsieur LaConne . . . ?'

Frau Kässler's eyes sparkled as she shook his hand. He was a handsome man. She had no doubt that he must have an agreeable penis. She wondered . . .

'Ah, my dear Monsieur LaConne – I have heard so much about you. Is it indeed true that it was you who first introduced Madelon to the pleasures of the flesh?'

Monsieur LaConne smiled modestly and nodded.

'She was an apt pupil, most advanced for her years. It was indeed a pleasure to give her her first fucking. The dear girl had a delightfully tight little cunt, as I remember, and a most winning way with her tongue. I always said she would go on to do great things, but I never thought that the next time we met, I would be coming to Friedenbourg to see her married to the Crown Prince!'

He took Frau Kässler's hand, and kissed it gallantly, letting his tongue run lightly over the flesh so that it teased and moistened it.

He looked up and saw that the Headmistress was gazing at him with lust in her eyes.

'My dear Headmistress, forgive me I pray you, for I have quite forgotten the niceties of protocol!' he exclaimed. 'It is so long since I visited your marvellous country. Would you, perhaps, do me the honour of allowing me to bugger you? I see that you have a pleasing backside, and doubt not that you have a fine, tight arsehole.'

Frau Kässler simpered, delighted at such silver-tongued flattery.

'To be sure, Monsieur, I should love to feel your cock stretching my arse. And indeed, I see that he is an eager fellow: I believe I can see him straining for his freedom inside your breeches!'

'For my part, Frau Kässler, I should dearly love to put my cock between your magnificent breasts, and watch my semen spurting out all over those creamy-white globes,' remarked Monsieur D'Abbeville.

'Your gallantry is charming, gentlemen,' replied Frau Kässler. And she began to unfasten her bodice, revealing the full extent of her ample and beautiful bosom. 'Would you care to fuck here, or in the comfort of my private chamber, where there is a most agreeable bed?'

'I myself,' replied Monsieur LaConne, 'can barely wait long enough for you to pull up the skirts of your dress. 'Twould be agony indeed to wait even moments longer to experience the divine tightness of your arse.'

Madelon's father agreed.

'Let it be here, Madame,' he replied. 'And if we are not too spent from our merry fucking, perhaps we could then adjourn to your private apartments, to share a little more wholesome pleasure before lunch? Mayhap your assistant, Signora Delmonico, might agree to join us? I noticed as we arrived that her breasts and thighs grow more comely with each day that passes. But for now, Frau Kässler, I see that you have a rather fine tigerskin rug beside your hearth. Would that not provide us with comfort enough for our enjoyment?'

The Headmistress, overwhelmed by her guests'

eagerness to enjoy her, pulled her large, creamy-white titties out of the prison of her bodice. With an exclamation of delight, Monsieur LaConne sprang forward and seized handfuls of the soft flesh. How it overflowed his hands, how it seemed to invite lips and tongue and teeth . . .

'My dear Joseph,' he exclaimed. 'I begin to wonder if I have chosen aright – for these titties are truly magnificent.'

Monsieur D'Abbeville unfastened the silver button which held together the Headmistress's skirt at the waistband, and let the garment fall in soft folds about her feet. As ever, she was naked underneath – for how can a Headmistress command the respect of her pupils if she does not practise what she preaches?

Monsieur D'Abbeville gave Frau Kässler's back-side a hearty and appreciative slap, which made the creamy flesh quiver and marble pink and white.

'Marcel, you have chosen magnificently,' he declared. 'And I swear that if there is spunk left in my balls after I have paid homage to Madame's breasts, I too shall enjoy the pleasure-palace of her arse.'

Naked and eager, Frau Kässler lay down on her side on the tigerskin rug. She watched in stiff-nippled anticipation as her two distinguished guests took off their formal morning coats, gloves and polished boots, unbuttoned their trousers and revealed their nakedness to her.

'Messieurs,' she cried. 'I had forgotten what magnificent pricks you have. Such wonderful, twin delights . . .'

Monsieur D'Abbeville was already on his knees beside Frau Kässler, stroking and kneading her breasts; whilst Monsieur LaConne slid his hand up the backs and sides of her thighs, and ran his fingers over her arse-cheeks, delaying the magical moment when he would wrench them apart and enjoy the first sight of her arsehole.

Frau Kässler scarcely knew what to do. She longed to move – to writhe, to roll about, to open herself up to these gentlemen's ministrations: but she knew that she could not. For if she should roll on to her belly, the better to offer up her arse, she would deprive herself of the wondrous sensation of having her titties stimulated; and if she should roll on to her back, favouring her breasts, she would lose the joy of having her arse stroked and caressed.

At last, her prayers were answered. For the two gentlemen, understanding her plight and their own, sought a way in which all three of them might take their pleasure at the same time. They gently raised her up, so that she was on her hands and knees on the tigerskin rug, the tiger's head staring glassy-eyed and open-mawed from beneath her pendulous breasts.

Monsieur D'Abbeville masturbated his penis for a little while, then thrust it into Frau Kässler's mouth. She sucked on it like a hungry babe, eager for the strange milk which she knew would gush forth plenteously from this surreal breast. His hands were on her nipples, pinching them, pulling at them as though he were milking a cow; and she would have cried out for the pain and pleasure of it, had she not been half-suffocated by the prick thrusting eagerly down her throat.

Now he was withdrawing from her, before he had even spunked off. She felt resentful. Why was he depriving her of the joy of his orgasm?

But he withdrew only to attack once again. Now

he was pulling at her massive breasts, pulling them forward and thrusting his penis between them. It was hot and she could feel the blood pulsing through it; he was fucking her to the very rhythm of life . . .

Not to be outdone in ingenuity, Monsieur LaConne took hold of Frau Kässler's thighs and eased them gradually apart, the better to play with the hot, moist delights between her arse-cheeks and cunt-lips. She groaned with pleasure as she felt his fingers sliding in between her cunt-lips, searching out the throbbing button of her clitoris, whilst the other hand, bolder still, crept down from her cunt, slid along the furrow between her thighs, and found a haven between her arse-cheeks.

'My dear Frau Kässler,' exclaimed Monsieur LaConne, 'you have the most magnificently tight arsehole! I yearn to be inside you . . .'

Without further ado, Marcel LaConne placed the tip of his engorged penis against the puckered amber rose of her arsehole, and pushed home with energy and determination. Frau Kässler writhed in pleasure as the very tip of Monsieur LaConne's penis managed to penetrate her, and with a second, stronger thrust, he was at last within her. His hardness felt huge, magnificent, primeval; and his fingers were still on her clitty, rubbing, teasing, tormenting.

Her arsehole, which she had kept virgin-tight yet wonderfully supple through careful exercise, yielded with delicious difficulty to the invader. Frau Kässler began to imagine herself as some delicate young virgin, naked and alone in a dark primeval forest. Suddenly, she was set upon by the ravening beasts of the forest. Sabre-toothed tigers . . . magnificent and terrifying . . . with saliva dripping hungrily from their cruel, yellowed fangs . . .

They were hungry. They were going to tear her apart, unless . . .

She offered herself to them, opening up her most secret places to them. They sniffed the air, warily, but with excitement. Could they smell the scent of her womanhood, her readiness, her own excitement?

And they were upon her now, accepting what she offered, but on their own terms. Their pricks were huge, barbed, capable of inflicting terrible injuries. They wanted to fuck her as they would fuck their own tigresses, biting into the back of her neck and making the blood flow; thrusting their hardness into her with no thought of her pain. She was too weak, too frail, too human! She could not withstand such an ordeal!

She tried to escape, but it was too late. The first of the tigers had knocked her to her knees on the jungle floor, and strange tropical plants were conspiring to hold her there, to forbid her any moment. Lianas and vines were twining round her wrists and ankles like weird hands, gripping her, making her open up her flesh to her violators, forcing her to stay and bear what was to happen to her.

The first tiger's penis entered her, brutally, from behind, and she felt the tiny, sharp barbs abrading her sensitive flesh, invading her intimacy, forcing her body to experience pleasure when her mind could think only of pain.

She felt sharp teeth in her throat, and the blood began to flow. She would surely die . . .

As Monsieur LaConne buggered her, she felt her orgasm rising up from the very depths of her. With a muffled cry, she came; and Monsieur D'Abbeville's spunk jetted down her throat, half-choking her.

Seconds later, Monsieur LaConne came into her arse, filling her with his foaming semen.

Afterwards, they lay together for a little while on the tigerskin rug, enjoying the sensations of wild beasts, lazing in the tropical shade. After some time, Monsieur D'Abbeville lit a cigar and began to stroke Frau Kässler's amiable flank, thoughtfully and with a wicked glint in his eye.

'Shall we adjourn to your apartments, Madame? You have, after all, promised us a tour of your most intimate places . . .'

'Certainly, gentlemen!' Frau Kässler bent and kissed her guest's pricks, playfully and with a touch of mischievousness. 'But pray do not exhaust yourselves; for as you know, tonight you have an audience with Mademoiselle Madelon at Castle Amor.'

That evening, the road which wound up the hillside from the centre of Friedenheim to Castle Amor was choked with vehicles: humble farm-carts, landaus and surreys drawn by high-stepping thoroughbreds, and even a sprinkling of the new-fangled motor-cars, chugging noisily up the winding mountain road.

For tonight was the Grand Ball to celebrate the selection of Prince Albrecht's wife-to-be; and guests from all over the principality had been invited to the Castle to take part in the celebrations. Even lowly farmers and their wives had been called to Castle Amor; for, unlike their cousins in other parts of the crumbling Hapsburg Empire, Friedenbourg's citizens enjoyed a high degree of equality and autonomy.

Inside the castle, all was a blur of activity. Journalists and dignitaries mingled in the Grand Hall, their ladies dressed in their most sophisticated and erotic outfits: dresses made from diaphanous gauzy fabric, through which the contours of the body could clearly be seen; blouses cut low above high-waisted corsets, so that the breasts were offered like rare sweetmeats on a platter; dresses with circles cut out of the fabric, to reveal bare breasts or buttocks; dresses slashed from ankle to waist, baring glossy pubic curls or shaven cunts; and women with close-cropped hair, dressed in mannish leather, with tight breeches slashed at the groin to allow tantalising glimpses of their moist pink cunts.

In her apartments, Alex was helping Madelon to prepare herself for the evening's celebrations.

'Shall I wear the midnight-blue velvet, or the rose-pink silk? I just can't decide . . . Oh, Alex! I'm so excited!'

She held the two dresses up against her, and Alex nodded towards the blue velvet: a tight-waisted gown with transparent net over the breasts and open panel at the front.

'This one, Madelon,' she decided. 'It shows off your breasts and cunny so beautifully. And you simply must wear the new diamond clitty-ring the Prince has given you.'

Madelon sat down on the edge of the bed, with her legs apart, and took out her plain gold clitty-ring whilst Alex went over to the mantelpiece and took down a small silver box, in which the diamond clitty-ring lay on a bed of black velvet.

She knelt down in front of Madelon, who obligingly held her cunt-lips apart so that Alex could find her clitoris more easily. With a little effort, Alex succeeded in slipping the ring through Madelon's clitty and clicking it into place.

The ring was studded with diamonds and from its

centre hung a single diamond on a long golden chain, which hung pendulum-like between her thighs. As it swung to and fro, it exerted the most delicious pressure on her clitty, almost making her swoon for the pleasure of it.

Alex was just bending to kiss Madelon's clitty, when there was a knock at the door. The maid ran to open it, and was followed back into the room by Monsieur LaConne and Monsieur D'Abbeville.

'Father! Monsieur LaConne!' cried Madelon, leaping up from the bed and rushing to embrace her father, who was by no means indifferent to the subtle pressure of his daughter's breasts against the starched front of his evening shirt.

'My dear daughter, you are looking wonderful!' cried Monsieur D'Abbeville, wiping a tear of joy and pride from the corner of his eye. 'Is she not, Marcel?'

'Indeed she is, Joseph. And grown so tall and beautiful, too! Why, I well recall the day, so little time ago, when you asked me to perform that most responsible and pleasurable of duties: the taking of your daughter's virginity.'

'Ah yes,' reminisced Monsieur D'Abbeville. 'She was so eager, and yet so naive. And I watched with such unparalleled joy as you laid her down upon her bed and pierced her womanhood. You have been a true friend to my family, Marcel. I know that it is in great part the wisdom which you have imparted to my daughter which has enabled her to achieve such glowing success.'

'Will you not fuck me again, Monsieur?' pleaded Madelon. 'For I so long to feel your semen flowing out of me, as it did that first evening. I long to feel your hardness thrusting into me, as it did that very first time.'

With tears of nostalgia in his eyes, Monsieur LaConne unbuttoned the front of his dress trousers and pulled out his prick, which was every bit as beautiful and as serviceable as Madelon remembered it. He bade her lie on the edge of the bed, and spread and lift her legs.

Supporting her thighs with his strong hands, Marcel LaConne thrust into Madelon's cunt. The diamond ring moved in her clitoris, causing both of them the most exquisite sensations; and it was not long before they melted in a mutual tribute.

Madelon wished him to fuck her again, but her father reminded her of her duties. 'My dear girl,' he said, 'you have such a night of fucking ahead of you that you must marshall your strength and lusts. There are ordeals still left for you to perform, and you would not wish to disappoint the Prince.'

When, a few minutes later, the Prince's Chamberlain came to escort her to the Great Hall, Madelon had wiped away her tears of nostalgia and donned her gown of midnight-blue velvet. Her large, firm breasts gleamed like twin moons in the candlelight as she descended the stairs to the Great Hall, where her Prince and her future subjects awaited her.

The dark, hooded figure walked swiftly and silently up the road which led to the city of Friedenheim, leading his bay mare behind him. At his side walked a blonde girl, the steely glint in her eyes belying the softness of her body and femininity of her attire.

The hooded figure stopped, and turned towards the girl. There was doubt in his eyes.

'Perhaps I was mistaken. Perhaps I should turn

back. I mean them no harm. There is no urgency. There is still time to forget this foolish plan . . .'

The girl laughed, a harsh, hollow laugh which seemed to crackle through the summer night like unseasonable frost, ground beneath the heel.

'Are you no man? Are you afraid of this so-called Prince, who is no prince at all? Are you afraid of this mere slip of a girl who stands beside him, smiling and simpering and hiding the pride and malice in her heart? She hates me, and she has robbed me of what is rightfully mine. For years, the false Prince has robbed you of what is yours. Will you not now take what is yours by right? Or are you, as I feared, less than a man?'

The hooded figure rounded on her. When he spoke, it was coldly and quietly, almost a whisper – and yet there was anger in his voice.

'No man – or woman – calls me coward and lives.'

The blonde girl was undaunted.

'Then prove to me that you are no coward. Prove it to me, and enjoy my favours for ever more.'

Without a word of reply, the hooded figure turned and kept on trudging down the road towards Friedenheim. Beneath the hood, his face was grim with resolution.

5 An Uninvited Guest

Madelon was without a doubt the belle of the ball. All those who met her were charmed by her. Those who begged of her to fuck with them were not disappointed; she sent none away unsatisfied, and her public exhibitions of fucking sent the guests into rapturous applause.

At last, just before midnight, the Prince stood to make his speech of welcome.

'My lords, ladies, citizens and honoured guests,' he began. 'As you know, the lady Madelon has proved herself worthy indeed to be the wife of a Crown Prince, and I for one can testify to the skill of her gentle hands and tight cunt. We are to be married in two weeks' time, after the completion of the final ceremony.'

By his side, Madelon frowned. No one had told her about any additional ceremonies. Surely her contest with Hilde had been the end of it? She listened attentively, anxious to know more.

'We have decided,' continued the Prince, 'to revive an ancient custom of this principality; one which has fallen into disuse over the last few generations, but one which I am sure you – as loyal citizens – will agree is a charming and valuable one.

'Custom decrees that the Princess elect shall be

83

introduced to a selection of the lowliest of the male citizens of Friedenheim, whose names shall be chosen by ballot. She shall then be required to perform any sexual acts which these citizens demand of her.

'At the end of the period stipulated (which shall be not longer than seven days), provided that she has performed her sexual duties adequately, she shall be crowned Princess and we shall be married. I feel sure that my dear fiancée Madelon will agree with me that this is a chivalrous and charitable custom; and one which will give her ample scope to reveal the generous and affectionate disposition for which she is justly renowned.'

Quite amazed by what she had heard, Madelon nevertheless nodded and smiled, wondering what the Prince had meant by the 'lowliest citizens' of Friedenheim.

Fortunately, Madelon was not entirely unaccustomed to poverty – for the Conservatoire was active in providing volunteers to work at the charitable houses which had been set up throughout the city to provide sexual comfort to the poorest of its citizens. These houses, run by the Sisters of Carnal Pleasure, had given Madelon and several other prefects their first experiences of Friedenheim's lower orders, so Madelon felt reasonably confident about her preparedness for this new and unexpected ordeal.

'The four chosen men will be presented to you tomorrow morning, my dear,' the Prince addressed Madelon, 'so I trust you will sleep soundly tonight and will be well rested by the morning.'

He kissed her a fond goodnight, and she left the hall with Alex, her mind still reeling from the Prince's revelations.

Madelon spent a troubled night, in which she dreamed of hordes of coal-black savages, their oiled flesh gleaming in the moonlight. They were advancing towards her, and as they got nearer to her, she saw that their pricks were hugely erect and dripping semen from their engorged tips.

She tried to run away, but could not; for the weight of the crown on her head was so great that she could scarcely move beneath it. She put her hands to her brow and tried to remove it, but it seemed stuck fast.

Looking back, she saw that the savages were closing in on her. Some were masturbating furiously, and all at once she saw their mouths open in fierce glee and their glistening black pricks shoot great floods of semen at her. As it touched her skin, she felt it burn; and her clitoris began to throb. She knew then that she would have to fuck every one of these fearsome savages before she would be freed from the terrible tyranny of her unwholesome desire.

She awoke, to find that she was not alone in her bed. Alex had crept in beside her in the night, and was gently stroking the little pink buttons of her nipples. It was a soft and welcoming way to awake, and Madelon kissed Alex gratefully, reaching down and thrusting her fingers between Alex's thighs. Between her legs, Alex was dripping wet.

'Oh Alex, you bad girl!' squealed Madelon, delightedly. 'You've been wanking, and you never even asked me to join in! See, you can't hide the truth from me, you little minx – your snatch is as wet as anything.'

Alex's cheeks reddened with embarrassment.

'You were asleep . . . and I looked at your naked body and you were so beautiful, and . . . and I thought you couldn't possibly be interested in fucking with me, and . . . oh! Madelon! That feels so delicious! You truly do have magic in your fingers . . .'

Madelon rolled over and slid open the drawer of a little Louis XV escritoire which stood beside her bed. Inside lay a variety of interesting sex-toys, with which Friedenbourg's princesses had passed many a happy hour in innocent pleasure.

She selected what she was looking for, and took it out of the drawer.

'What on earth . . . ? What *have* you got there, Madelon?' gasped Alex, who was, in truth, still rather naive and inexperienced, despite all the best endeavours of her friend and the entreaties of Frau Kässler.

'Why, what does it look like, you silly goose? It's a double dildo – what did you think it was? Now, Alex, if you'd be kind enough to lick my clitoris just a little, so my juices start to flow . . . Yes, yes, that's it; just a *little* harder, perhaps . . .'

Alex licked Madelon so beautifully that she was afraid she would come before she had had a chance to pleasure her friend. So she gently pushed Alex away, ignoring her protestations, and slid a finger into her own cunt.

'That's better', she declared. 'Nice and slippery now, thanks to you.'

She took hold of the double-headed dildo, which was truly a monster of a thing. Carved from wood, it represented two enormously engorged pricks, each seven or eight inches long, and placed back to back. Madelon slipped one of the two wooden pricks gently but lasciviously into Alex's cunt, and then lay down on her back on the bed.

'Fuck me, Alex,' she entreated. 'Come and fuck me, just like you were a man and I was a little virgin you'd just brought home to seduce.' She knew how much Alex enjoyed playing these little games, so she went on: 'Now, I'm a little girl who's run away from home, and you're an unscrupulous pimp who finds me begging for bread on a street corner. It's obvious that I'm a little virgin, and I've no idea of the games that men and women play together. I'm not from Friedenbourg, you see . . . I'm from some terribly backward country, where only married people fuck, and then only after dark.

'Well, you've brought me home to your apartment, and you've drugged me to make me easier to seduce. You don't want to rape me – that would be too easy. But you can't wait to get your fat cock into my tight little virgin hole. You just love fucking little girls, and making them writhe with pleasure underneath you.

'I'm protesting a little now – I'm afraid. I don't know what you're going to do to me, but you've asked me to take off my knickers, and I'm afraid. Oh yes, yes, Alex: stroke my breasts, suck my nipples – make me feel how much I want to be fucked. Now show me what it is you've got between your legs: such a pretty plaything! Make me want it; make me want to feel its hardness forcing its way into me, making me a woman though I'm hardly more than a child . . .'

Unable to bear the suspense any longer, and overcome with the most terrible pangs of lust, Alex pressed the point of the dildo against Madelon's cunny-hole, and thrust home, strongly and without gentleness. An electric sensation of exquisite

87

pleasure coursed through both young women's cunts.

'Oh yes, yes!' cried Madelon. 'Fuck me, fuck me, fuck me, my darling Alex!'

Alex rode her like a charger, making her gallop every inch of the way towards her orgasm. And as they came together, and collapsed, groaning with pleasure, on to the bed, Madelon truly believed that she was a little girl, seduced by a wicked pimp in some backstreet whorehouse.

Afterwards, they got up and bathed, ready for the arrival of Madelon's chosen suitors. Still she knew nothing about them, save that they would all be relatively poor, and that they would range in age from the very young to the very old.

At nine o'clock, after breakfast, Madelon went down to the robing-room, where Alex and Frau Agathe dressed her in a fine gown of diaphanous primrose-yellow muslin, overlaid with pearls. She wore no undergarments, for the future Crown Princess must show the perfect example of sensuality to her subjects; and her nipples were each encased in little golden sheaths, which protruded through small holes in her bodice.

She was taken to the Salon of a Thousand Kisses, to await the arrival of her visitors.

They arrived promptly an hour later, were each introduced in turn by the Lord Chamberlain, and then sent away to await a visit from the princess, later on in the day or week.

First to be introduced was a man Madelon already knew well: Thorold, the muscular blacksmith who had often visited the Conservatoire when the horses needed to be shod. Many was the happy hour Madelon and her friends had spent with him, sucking his big hard prick and watching the semen bubble as it spurted out of him on to the glowing coals of his furnace. She sighed with relief, knowing that she could happily give Thorold his heart's desire; and she promised to visit him later on that day.

The next visitor was very different. He was an old man, Ludwig Kreiss, rather deaf and on crutches. It transpired that he was from one of the outlying villages, where he had been a potter until his hands had become too crippled with arthritis to work.

Unable to kneel before her, the old man smiled toothlessly and bowed his head.

'What is your heart's desire, Herr Kreiss?'

The old man sighed, and his rheumy eyes filled with tears.

'I long to piss on your face, your eyes, your breasts, my Princess,' he replied. 'I yearn to piss into your cunt, also. And that shall give me more joy than all the fucking in the world.'

'Your desires shall be fulfilled,' replied Madelon. 'I shall come to you tonight, and do whatever you desire of me.'

The next visitor was also an old man; but this time he was not even outwardly respectable. Madelon realised immediately, from his filthy garb and lice-ridden hair, that this was an itinerant monk, one of the bizarre 'holy men' who passed through the principality from time to time, on their way back to Mother Russia.

He knelt before her, but Madeleine knew from the look upon his face that he was not cowed by her newfound royalty. The strange light in his eyes owed little to holiness or the purity of heavenly joy.

'My desire is this, my child,' he replied, in answer to her question. 'That you allow me to lay you down naked in the bank of stinging-nettles beside my forest cell, and yet not cry out for pain as I bugger you until my desire is sated. I desire also that you should taste the many leaden tongues of my whip, that I may purify your vile adulterous flesh with the purifying fire of pain. And then I shall run your body through with my carnal lance.'

White-faced but determined to show no sign of weakness, Madelon inclined her head in agreement. 'It shall be done.'

Only two more visitors. But what new horrors would they bring her? Was there no poor man in Friedenbourg who harboured natural desires towards her?

The fourth visitor struck terror into her heart. The black leather mask covered his face entirely, save for small holes for eyes, nose and mouth. His bare chest was criss-crossed with old battle-scars and he wore studded leather bands on his forearms. His only other garments were studded leather leggings, and kneeboots. He carried the symbol of his office in his arms: a mighty double-headed axe.

'What do you desire of me, Lord Executioner?' Madelon's voice trembled uncontrollably as she gazed into those fearsome, pitiless eyes.

'My desire is that you submit yourself to me utterly,' replied the masked man, fingering the blade of his axe. 'My desire is that you come to me when I summon you, and perform whatever task I ask of you. And that, should you fail, your forfeit is to submit to the wrath of my blade . . .'

Madelon stood in trembling silence for a moment, before marshalling her courage. 'It shall be as you desire it,' she said. 'But mark you: I shall not fail.'

She was almost in tears as the door closed behind

him and she heard his footsteps fading away down the stone-paved hallway. She trembled as she wondered when he would call her, and what obscenities he would force her to subject herself to.

One last visitor. Would he, too, demand of her obedience or death?

'My lady, my name is Dieter Richtig, and I am a groom of His Highness the Prince's Royal Household. As you can see, I am a young man without any great experience or learning. All I ask of you is the chance to fuck you and return to you the pleasure which you will undoubtedly have given to me.'

Such gallantry raised Madelon's spirits immeasurably; and she could almost have kissed Dieter there and then. She eyed him up and down appreciatively. A tall youth, with dark hair and sparkling blue eyes, he returned her gaze with equal approbation.

Madelon felt a great wave of lust rising within her, and reached out and gently stroked the front of Dieter's riding-breeches. His prick swelled appreciatively within his tight pants, and the corners of his mouth twitched as he tried unsuccessfully to suppress a smile.

He knelt gallantly before Madelon, pulled open the sides of her skirt and kissed her naked pubis. A shudder of pleasure ran through her body, and she could not suppress a little gasp of joy.

'Until tomorrow, my dear Dieter,' she whispered to him. 'I shall come to you tomorrow, in the Prince's stables.'

Dieter took his leave and the doors of the Great Hall closed quietly behind him. Left alone in the silence, Madelon's thoughts did not dwell upon the terrors which awaited her, but upon the clear blue eyes and swelling prick of the young groom, Dieter Richtig.

Late that afternoon, Madelon ushered the first of her enforced guests into her private bedchamber. The old man, Kreiss, was almost overcome with the excitement of the moment, his feeble limbs trembling as he struggled to rid himself of his constricting clothes.

Madelon told herself that she must not flinch from her duty. Whatever the old man demanded of her, she must give him the fullest satisfaction. To fail in this ancient custom would be at the very least an outrage to protocol, and at the worst, perhaps Madelon would be sent back to the Conservatoire in disgrace! Although she was not especially attracted to Prince Albrecht, she could not face letting down her family and schoolfriends by failing at this last, paltry hurdle.

She sat down on the bed, naked save for the jewellery Albrecht had given her as an engagement present: the diamond necklet, the silver wrist and ankle-chains, and of course the exquisite diamond-drop clitty ring, whose divine heaviness excited Madelon's cunt to floods of fragrant juice, even in the face of such an unattractive sexual partner.

'What is your will, Herr Kreiss?' If she had hoped the old man would have forgotten his crazy desires and would make some more ordinary demand upon her, she was to be sorely disappointed.

'Princess, I would have you suck me to erection – no mean feat in itself, for as you can see I am an old man. And then, whilst my prick is still inside you, I shall piss into your delicate rosebud mouth. And you, my pretty little Princess, shall swallow it

92

down – all of it. And later, when I have recovered my spirits a little and we have taken tea here, in your bedroom, I shall piss into your tight little royal cunt.'

With an inner sigh of resignation, Madelon got on to her knees before the old man and took his penis into her mouth. It was flaccid, wrinkled, uninspired and uninspiring. Surely all the sucking in the world would not raise the dead . . . ?

She sucked at him for a full ten minutes, to little good effect. Then the old man bent and hissed in her ear:

'I want to see you piss, Princess. Here, in front of me.'

He reached under the bed and dragged out the china chamberpot which was always there for the occupant's comfort; and he placed it in front of Madelon.

The look in his eyes was one of tyranny. Madelon knew that look meant: 'Do it now, or I shall tell the Prince how much you disappointed me.'

In despair, Madeleine squatted over the pot. Nothing happened. She was too inhibited. How could she piss in front of this hideous, toothless old man? Suddenly, he reached across and rubbed her clitty, very hard and very ruthlessly. She came to a sudden, brutal orgasm which sent her cunt into such reckless spasms that she quite forgot herself, and her bladder emptied itself spontaneously into the chamberpot.

To Madelon's surprise, she realised that the old man's prick was swelling and hardening at the sight of her pissing into the pot. By the time she had finished, he was hard and ready for her.

Without further ado, Herr Kreiss sat down on the

edge of the bed and made Madelon kneel before him and take his hardness into her mouth. It tasted strong – a harbinger of what was to come, Madelon thought grimly to herself. She licked at him and wondered if she might somehow manage to bring him to such a peak of excitement that he would forget his foolish plan, and instead submit to the joys of orgasm.

But to her dismay, a flood of foul-tasting liquid suddenly filled her mouth. He was pissing down her throat! She half-choked and tried to pull away, but his claw-like hands held her fast with surprising strength and he would not let her go free. He forced her to swallow every drop.

Afterwards, he rang the bell for the maid and forced Madelon to drink English tea with him, out of fine bone-china cups, whilst his skeletal fingers wandered over her body, invading her most secret places. Soon, he promised her with a disgusting leer, he would lay her down on the bed and piss into her cunt . . .

After he had gone, Alex washed out Madelon's mouth and cunt with rosewater, in an attempt to erase the memory of the hideous old man. Scarcely had Madelon made herself presentable once more when there was a knock at the door.

It was a messenger from Brother Grigor.

'You must go to him in the Castle chapel at midnight,' Alex explained to her, somewhat breathlessly. 'He will take you to his cell in the forest, there to do with you as he will. Oh, Madelon – are you sure that you have not done the wrong thing? There is still time to withdraw, to go back to our old life at the Conservatoire . . .'

Madelon patted Alex's hand companionably.

'One down, and only four to go,' she said with forced joviality. 'And once these ordeals are over, the rest will be plain sailing. Once I am married to the Prince, I shall be free to fuck with whomsoever I please. Don't worry, Alex: I'll be careful.'

She placed delicate kisses on the tips of Alex's breasts, running her tongue over the firm white flesh.

'No, Alex. Shall we rest a little while upon the bed before my next trial?'

And she took Alex into her arms and laid her gently upon the bed, stroking her thighs very softly and delicately until they opened like an exotic flower, revealing the fragrant spring of nectar within the heart of the petals.

Just before midnight, Madelon slung her velvet cloak over her shoulders and walked through the Castle grounds towards the chapel.

The little gothic building was in darkness, no glimmer of light visible within through the elegant stained-glass windows. Madelon stood on tiptoe and peered through the glass, but there was no sign of movement within. Perhaps she was early?

The sound of the town hall bell tolling midnight, down in the centre of the town, interrupted Madelon's thoughts. She moved round to the main door of the chapel and turned the handle.

The door opened with a sinister creak. There was nothing to be seen inside, no sign of movement. She was just about to turn and go back outside to wait for the monk, when a voice behind her whispered:

'Good evening, my child. I am so glad that you decided to accept my terms . . .'

It happened very quickly. The stench of filth overwhelmed her as strong hands seized her and ropes burned her skin, biting into her wrists and ankles. A filthy gag was stuffed into her mouth, to stifle her screams, and she felt arms enfolding her, lifting her up, carrying her outside.

She was slung like a sack of potatoes over the back of Brother Grigori's mule, and they set off out of the Castle gates and down an overgrown path towards the forests which covered the northern slopes and hills behind Friedenheim.

The monk's cell was a cold, damp cave cut into the rock-face. Water was running down the walls, and as Brother Grigori lit the tallow candle, Madelon caught sight of something dark and sleek, scuttling away into the shadows.

'My pretty one . . .' sighed the Brother, untying Madelon's ankles but keeping tight hold of her wrists, to stop any attempt to run away. 'I shall so much enjoy our little assignation, I am sure of it. Come now, let me see the full beauty of your nakedness.'

The monk produced a sharp, bone-handled hunting knife from his belt. Madelon flinched as the blade caught the flickering candlelight, sending out threatening glints of brightness. But he did not harm her. He merely used the knife to cut away her clothes and bare her creamy-white flesh.

He ran his hands over Madelon's helpless body. He was very close to her now, and she could smell the rancid stench of his unwashed body. She began to imagine what manner of vermin lived in that wild, unkempt hair and those filthy clothes. His breath was hot and sour on her face as he stole a kiss, forcing his tongue into her mouth, pressing his burgeoning hardness against her. He was evidently enjoying her discomfiture.

He took hold of the rope which bound Madelon's wrists together, and dragged her out of the cave and into a little clearing in the forest. At one side was a bank of stinging nettles . . .

She tried to cry out, but the gag prevented her from making more than a muffled sound, stifling her fear. Brother Grigori pushed her forward and she stumbled. Unable to save herself with her arms, she plunged forward on to her belly, only inches from the nettles.

The brother showed her no mercy. He picked her up and threw her, back first, into the bank of nettles. It felt as though a thousand needles were entering her flesh, enraging and inflaming her senses, burning into her. Madelon was in an ecstasy of pain and torment. She tried to get to her feet, but with her hands tied behind her she was utterly helpless; and each movement caused her new agonies.

Brother Grigori was laughing like a madman. Now he was untying his knotted rope sash, and pulling his habit off over his head. His filthy body was covered with matted hair. He approached Madelon, his massive penis thrusting at her like some weapon of war. Madelon knew she was no match for him.

He bent down and picked up something. Something long and black and sinister, with long black tails, tipped with something small but heavy . . . beads of lead? He was going to whip her with his cat-o'-nine-tails!

Madelon's body arched in pain as the first blow struck her across her breasts. Inwardly she was screaming, but she could make no sound, for her throat was half closed by the filthy rag. Again, again,

again. He was revelling in her pain, her discomfiture. The thongs of the cat were thrashing her cunt now, forcing the lips apart in spite of her terror and pain; striking against the unruly clitoris which sprang to attention in defiance of her fear.

He dropped the lash and threw himself upon her, almost crushing her with his bulk and running her through at the first attempt. His prick distended her cunt, stretching its walls painfully, though her cunt was wet with her own unwilling pleasure. She could feel his balls slapping up against her arse-cheeks.

Madelon felt herself drifting off into a haze of pleasure and pain, where nothing seemed real. A phantasmagorical world in which dark shapes moved soundlessly, their fiery tongues licking her flesh to an unendurable peak of terror and ecstasy.

He brought her to orgasm three times before at last he released the mighty tide of his sperm into her violated cunt. And then, silently, he left her lying in the middle of the bank of nettles, and walked away into the darkness, towards his cave.

Madelon lay in silent helplessness for a few moments, hardly knowing what she must do. Then there was a rustling in the undergrowth, and she looked up to see a familiar figure.

Thorold! Her old friend Thorold the blacksmith had come to save her, just in the nick of time! He at least would keep her safe from the marauding wolves.

'Good evening, Madelon!' cried Thorold, with a broad smile. Madelon saw that his breeches were unbuttoned, and he was cradling his stiffened prick in his massive, bear's-paw hand. 'Such an evening's sport you have given me, my sweet! To see the Christian charity of yon brother quite moved me to tears. Twice the sight of your sport brought me to my pleasure, and yet the fellow is still as hard and as eager as ever!'

Madelon realised, with a sinking feeling, that she was not going to be released quite as simply and quickly as she had thought.

The blacksmith took the gag from Madelon's mouth with a flourish.

'Cry out as much as you please, my dear,' he cried, 'for no one will hear you save Brother Grigori, and I think your cries will only add to his pleasure. Yes, cry out all you please: 'twill do you a power of good to have some pain in your fucking. You young ladies of the Conservatoire are far too refined and gently bred!'

Conceding defeat, Madelon offered no resistance as the blacksmith mounted her and rode her like an expert horseman to another unwilling orgasm.

As his parting gift to her, he dragged her out of the nettles and forced her to her knees before him, tweaking the tips of her breasts so hard and so expertly that she climaxed even before he spurted his final load into her mouth.

It was a sore and wiser Madelon who made her way back to Castle Amor in the grey light of an approaching dawn.

The following morning, Alex tut-tutted like a mother hen over Madelon's still-bruised and reddened flesh. Madelon winced as her friend smoothed the soothing ointment over her breasts and buttocks – not only with pain, but with the humiliating memory of what had happened to her the previous night, in the forest.

'How could he?' cried Alex, full of righteous indignation. 'To drag you into the forest and treat you like an animal. And then for Thorold to abandon you to the wolves and brigands who roam the forest at night . . . ! And to think he seemed such a friend to us all at the Conservatoire.'

Madelon did not reply. She was thinking of the summons which had just come from the Executioner. The message had been written in blood on a scrap of parchment, summoning her to the old dungeons of the castle, which until the time of Albrecht's grandfather, had been used to torture and imprison anyone who displeased the Prince.

And now they were going to be used to torture and imprison her . . .

She put the finishing touches to her toilette, gave Alex a sisterly peck on the cheek, and set off for the dungeons.

It was a hot, sunny day, and it seemed strange to be descending the long, winding stone staircase, into a world of menace. As she reached the bottom of the steps, a sudden gust of wind blew out her candle, plunging her into darkness.

A voice from within the depths of the dungeon spoke to her, slowly and softly:

'Come in, my darling Madelon. I've been expecting you . . .'

She took two steps forward, then stumbled and had to support herself by clinging on to the wall. Suddenly a light flickered in the gloom, and she blinked in the unexpected brightness.

The light from the lantern spread its eerie orange glow through the damp dungeon, illuminating dripping walls and the horrible instruments of torture hanging on them. Madelon gasped as she saw the rack before her, wound up ready for its next passenger. She had no idea that such horrors could have persisted into the modern world. Was the Executioner planning to use these terrible things on her?

The Executioner opened the door of the iron maiden, and Madelon gazed with horror at the array of fearsome spikes inside. He turned his masked face towards her, and there was a strange light in his eyes.

'Will you submit yourself utterly to me?'

Madelon shivered. Her voice trembling, she replied: 'I will.'

'And if you displease me, you realise that you shall risk the ultimate punishment?' He fingered the cruel double blade of his axe.

'I . . . I understand. What is it that you require of me?'

'I require, my little one, that you and I together shall share the kinship of sweet pain. Pain that I shall administer, and you shall experience. Is that not a fair division of spoils?' He did not wait for her reply.

The Executioner placed a leather halter over her head, with an iron bit which he pushed between her lips. Madelon felt the cold iron mouthpiece pressing down her tongue, effectively gagging her.

Then he took down from the wall a set of heavy iron shackles, which he closed about her wrists. Leading from them was a long chain which reached to her ankles, and joined on to two heavy anklets. They clicked round her ankles and she was a prisoner of her heavy chains. What would he do with her now?

The Executioner released a rope which hung down the wall, and a large hook began to be lowered gradually from the ceiling. It was made from coarse iron, heavily rusted and obviously very old. Before Madelon realised what he was doing, the Executioner had threaded its point through the middle link of her manacles, and was beginning to heave on the rope.

Madelon suddenly realised, as the rope jerked her arms above her head, what the Executioner was doing. He was going to use the hook to pull her off the ground, suspend her from the ceiling so that she would be truly at the mercy of his own fiendish amusement.

She cried out as the hook rose higher and her feet were jerked off the ground. She felt as though her arms were being wrenched out of their sockets. Within seconds she was well clear of the ground, and spinning slowly and uncontrollably on the end of the hook.

The Executioner secured the rope at the wall, and came over to inspect his prize. He seemed well pleased, and began to run his leather-gloved hands over Madelon's flesh. The rough-seamed gloves excited her, in spite of the terrible discomfort of hanging there, suspended by her arms; and Madelon gave a muffled sigh of pleasure as the Executioner's gloved finger toyed with her clitty-ring and probed deep into her cunt.

The next sensation was less pleasant; for the Executioner had taken something else down from the wall . . . Madelon gasped with pain, and blinked back sudden tears as the bunched chains struck her fragile flesh.

He struck her backside again and again, and she hung there, silent and impassive, utterly unable to defend herself against the Executioner's cruel assaults. She closed her eyes and tried to imagine herself elsewhere – anywhere but here; but the pain would not be blotted out.

Slowly and treacherously, the pain became heat, and the heat diffused a strange, insidious warmth through her entire body, stiffening her nipples and moistening her cunt. Slowly, unexpectedly, Madelon's pain was turning into the most exquisite pleasure . . .

At last he stopped beating her, and the chains fell silent at the Executioner's side. Madelon looked down and saw that he had unfastened the front of his trousers; and his magnificent prick was gleaming ghostly-white against the black leather.

She wanted to roar out her pleasure as he took a sword from the wall and turned it so that its hilt was towards her; then he thrust it home, deep into her backside, working it in and out whilst he twisted and turned the diamond-studded clitty-ring that governed every thought in her head, every beat of her heart. Sobbing with unwilling pleasure, she came in a flood of foaming cunt-juice.

He was lowering her down, down, towards the ground. Her feet were touching the ground, but there was no strength in them. She had not even the strength to stand unaided, and as he released her from the hook and chains, she fell unwillingly into the Executioner's arms.

He picked her up as though she were no more than a doll, and carried her over to the rack, the nightmare instrument of unbelievable torture. She was too weak to resist him now, and the insistent throbbing of her clitoris made her his consenting victim. She could not have denied him, even if her lips were not sealed by the halter and iron bit.

He bound her wrists and ankles to the rack, so that she lay splayed out like a starfish, naked and completely open to his every whim. He turned the handle, and the chains tightened, pulling her arms and legs further apart.

She wanted to scream out, 'No more, no more!', but her cries were silenced. Would he truly break her upon the rack? The pain in her shoulders and thighs was intense. No more, she could take no more . . .

And just as she was on the point of losing consciousness, he stopped turning the handle. She lay helpless beneath him as he climbed on to the rack and placed the tip of his penis against the entrance to her cunt.

The orgasm, when it came, was the most unimaginable blend of torment and ecstasy, and Madelon lost consciousness as her dark knight poured forth his tribute into her overflowing cunt.

When Madelon awoke, it was in the safety and comfort of her own bed, bathed and soothed with exotic unguents. Alex was waiting by her side, full of sisterly consideration.

'Are you all right, Madelon? I thought you would never come back to us! I . . . I was afraid you might die!'

Madelon laughed.

'Don't be a silly goose, Alex. I'm made of sterner stuff than that. Only one more trial to undergo now, and my ordeals will be at an end.'

Secretly, she was wondering if, behind those clear blue eyes, Dieter Richtig was concealing some black secret which she could only guess at . . .

She went to the stables that afternoon, when

Dieter was busily curry-combing the Prince's favourite stallion.

'He is a very fine fellow, is he not, my lady?'

'Call me Madelon. After all, we are going to be friends, are we not, Dieter?'

She stroked the horse's flank appreciatively. 'He is indeed a fine stallion, and mettlesome, too. It takes a strong hand to command him. Indeed, it is said that only a royal master can subdue him. And yet he stands his ground for you, and seems even to love you. You must be a very remarkable groom, Dieter Richtig.'

Dieter turned his blue eyes on Madelon, and she felt her nipples stiffen with desire as he laid his strong hand on her shoulder.

'You need not fuck with me, Madelon – not if you don't wish to. I think it's a stupid custom. Whatever you want me to say to the Council of Ministers, I'll say it.'

Madelon looked at him quizzically, unsure how to take this chivalrous gesture.

'Don't you want me, Dieter? Don't you want to fuck me, to lick my cunt? Wouldn't you like me to suck your cock and drink down your semen?'

He turned on his heel, and threw himself at her feet, kissing her thighs and putting his hand up her skirt to stroke her pubic curls.

'More than anything, Madelon. More than anything, I want to fuck you.'

Madelon smiled and raised him to his feet, then led him by the hand into the sweet-smelling barn, where the warm, soft straw would provide a fine bed for their lovemaking.

When she left, a few hours later, Madelon knew

that, whatever else happened, she would never be able to keep away from Dieter Richtig.

That night, a Council of Ministers met in the Great Hall, and all of Madelon's suitors came to pay their respects and testify to her charitable nature and sexual prowess.

When it was at an end, and Madelon had made an assignation with Dieter for the following day, the Prince was about to proclaim the date of the royal wedding when the doors of the throne room burst open and a terrified messenger scuttled in, throwing himself at the Prince's feet.

'What is the meaning of this?' thundered the Prince.

'Your Highness, a terrible thing . . . There is a visitor outside, claiming . . .'

'Speak, man! Have you lost your tongue?'

'Oh, your Royal Highness, it is so terrible, I cannot tell!'

'I can speak for myself.'

The voice came from the open doorway, where a tall figure stood, wrapped in a long woollen cloak, his face shrouded by a deep hood. Beside him stood Florence Desfarges, her face a picture of malicious glee.

'Let my face speak for me; for it cannot lie.'

The stranger took a few steps into the throne room, then reached up and pushed back the hood from his face.

It was a handsome face: blue-eyed, dark-haired, with a tiny birthmark just above his upper lip. The Prince stared at the stranger as though he had seen some terrible vision.

'A ghost!' he muttered hoarsely. 'Can a man see his own ghost . . . ? How can this be?'

'Your Highness, I am your brother,' said the stranger, his voice cutting through the heavy silence like a knife slicing through a taut thread. 'Your long-lost twin brother, Reinholdt.'

6   A Crisis in Friedenbourg

The whole principality was in an uproar. Overnight, the whole question not just of the royal wedding, but of the royal succession, had been cast into doubt.

There could be no doubt that Albrecht and Reinholdt – if such were his name – were brothers, for they were as alike as two peas in a pod. And it was certainly true that Albrecht had had a twin brother, kidnapped in infancy and long believed dead. Reinholdt claimed that he had been brought up by an old Swiss woman who told him she had found him abandoned on a hillside, and taken him in out of charity.

All his life, Reinholdt had lived as a poor man, without pretentions to wealth: a penniless writer of erotica, hounded by the Swiss authorities for his 'moral corruption'. Only now did he realise why he had felt so drawn to write of matters of the flesh . . .

It was not until he had seen Albrecht's photograph in all the newspapers that Reinholdt had been forced to question the truth of the old woman's story. In a frenzy of doubt, he had travelled back to the mountain village of his childhood, where the old woman still lived; and in tears she had confessed to him the story of his true birthright. He had been given to her by kidnappers whose plot had gone wrong, and who dared not return the child to his rightful parents, for fear of death.

She had taken him in, and brought him up as her own son.

Reinholdt had decided, there and then, to make the journey to Friedenbourg, and sold everything he owned to pay for his fare. At first, he had intended only to see his brother privately, and persuade him to bestow some modest settlement upon him, to ease the burden of his life.

And then he had met Florence Desfarges. She had shown him, most convincingly, that he ought not to cast off his birthright so easily. Why, might he not be the elder of the twin brothers? Might he – and not Albrecht – be the rightful heir to the Principality of Friedenbourg?

Albrecht and his ministers went into conference immediately. A state of emergency was proclaimed throughout the Principality. For the time being at least, there would be no royal wedding, and no coronation.

Madelon was bored. Being Crown Princess-Elect had begun to pall since she had discovered how much she preferred Dieter to Albrecht. And now she was being forced to sit through this boring Council of Ministers, listening to old men droning on about affairs of state.

Those were not the sort of affairs young Madelon was interested in . . .

'If we accept that this man Reinholdt really is the missing prince . . .' began the Minister for Sexual Development.

'. . . As we indeed must,' interjected the Chancellor, 'since the man has brought authenticated documentary evidence with him. There is no disputing the signed confessions of his kidnappers.'

'Agreed.' The Minister nodded. 'But, even assuming that Reinholdt truly is a prince of the von Frieden dynasty, we have no way of determining which is the elder of the two princes, Albrecht or Reinholdt.'

'Then we must find a way. We must think quickly of a way to select the rightful heir to the throne, and present our findings to both princes before this day is out. For with every moment's delay, our enemies throughout the Empire will be plotting to overthrow our sovereignty and bring us back under the Hapsburg yoke.'

'Ah, the happy days of Empire,' sighed a wizened old courtier, half slumped in his chair at the end of the table. 'The Emperor was a fine young man, with a magnificent prick. Many were the times we fucked together in his hunting-lodge, deep in the forests near Vienna. Even now, my arsehole aches for him . . .'

A few of the older ministers shared his nostalgia for the old days; but the younger men guarded Friedenbourg's newfound sovereignty jealously. Nothing must happen to weaken the monarchy and threaten the principality's autonomy.

A heated discussion began, centring on some arcane point of constitutional law; but Madelon's attention was wandering. She was still thinking about Dieter.

The young groom had led her so gently to the barn, and unbuttoned her blouse so tenderly that she had felt like some priceless jewel, being unwrapped so that it could show its sparkle to the world for the first time. After the ordeals she had endured with

Herr Kreiss, Brother Grigori and the Executioner, it was almost impossible for her to believe that here was a young man who found her body attractive in a simple and sensual way, without the bizarre complications of violence and perversity.

As she stood there before him, naked to the waist, her first reaction had been to fall to her knees before him and worship his young, yearning manhood. She had kissed and stroked the front of his corduroy breeches; and would have pulled out his prick and blessed it with a thousand kisses, had he not prised her hands from his flies and put his strong arms round her, silencing her with a kiss upon the lips.

He lifted her up in his strong arms, and carried her over to the corner of the barn, into one of the empty horse-stalls. The floor retained the scent of horses, but it was clean and covered in dry, warm straw. He laid her down on this rustic bed, and then lay down beside her, stroking the tips of her breasts with reverential fingers.

Dieter propped her head up on a bale of straw, so that she could see what was happening at the other side of the barn. Left to its own devices, the fine bay stallion Dieter had been curry-combing had slipped its reins and wandered back inside the barn, attracted not only by the scent of fresh hay but by the infinitely more exciting scent of a mare in season.

The pretty little piebald mare was munching unconcernedly at a manger full of sweet hay, and scarcely noticed the stallion until he was behind her, nuzzling her flanks with his eager lips and tongue. Madelon watched in fascination as the stallion's penis began to swell to a tremendous length – like a stiff wooden baton, dancing with desire between his strong thighs. His massive testicles hung behind, taut and full of sperm.

Madelon began to wonder what it would feel like to be fucked by a stallion; to be crammed full of his engorged sex, ramming into her time and time again; to have that abundance of frothing sperm suddenly jet up into her tight little cunt . . .

Many a time, Signora Delmonico had taken the junior girls to see animals fucking. She had always said that it would promote a healthy growth of the libido; and Madelon could see now why she had set such store by it. She looked at the stallion's penis, and longed for her little cunt to be crammed to bursting with such smooth, swollen flesh; to have its hardness pressing against the neck of her womb. Dieter's fingers were stroking her flanks, teasing her nipples, as gently and as skilfully as he might stroke the flanks of his favourite mare. Madelon imagined Dieter as the stallion and herself as the little piebald mare, and gasped with delight as the stallion reared up on to his hind legs and his stiff prick sought an entrance into the female.

The mare whinnied with alarm, and bucked and tried to throw off her assailant. But the stallion's teeth held her fast, biting savagely at the back of her neck. Paradoxically, the harder he bit into her flesh, the more placid and amenable the mare became, as though she realised instinctively that his was a loving bite, the bite of sweet, sensual sex . . .

The stallion's prick at last found entrance to the mare's secret intimacy. His first thrust into her seemed never-ending . . . what a capacious cunt the mare must have! Madelon felt suddenly jealous of this submissive little mare, with her deep, silken-smooth cunt, which was giving her stallion so much pleasure.

Instinctively, Madelon reached out to her side and sought out Dieter's flies. The front of his breeches formed a little flap, fastened with four elkhorn buttons. Madelon struggled with them for a little while, and at last they gave way. She wriggled her hand inside the flap and was delighted to find that Dieter was wearing no underwear underneath his breeches.

His prick was long and firm, with a delightful upward-arching curve to it, like some ethereal bow, arching back to shoot out its pearly arrows.

The stallion neighed his pleasure as his bollocks tensed and shot their load into the mare, who whinnied as her cunt filled with his foaming tribute.

So abundant was the stallion's semen that, even before he withdrew his prick, pearly-white fluid bubbled out of the mare's cunt and trickled down her slender legs.

Madelon, entranced by the spectacle which Nature – and Dieter – had staged for her entertainment, rolled over on to her side, wriggled down in the straw and fastened her lips over the tip of Dieter's penis. It tasted sweet and smelt lightly of clean, fresh straw, and Madelon sucked greedily at it.

'Careful, careful . . .' warned Dieter. 'I am very excited already, my dear Madelon. If you suck me too hard, I shall spend and it will all be over too soon . . . oh, Madelon, it is too late! I am going to come!'

With a sigh of pleasure and despair, Dieter abandoned himself to Madelon's lips, flooding her willing mouth with his youthful sperm.

Afterwards, he lay back panting on the straw.

'Don't worry, Dieter: I'll soon have you hard

again,' Madelon assured him. And she produced a little bottle of scented oil from the pocket of her skirt. Then she unfastened her skirt and lay down beside him again, this time completely naked, save for the diamond-drop clitty-ring which sparkled temptingly between her creamy-white thighs.

She put a few drops of the oil into the palm of her hand, and then began gently to massage Dieter's penis and testicles with it.

'Bergamot to soothe and seduce the senses,' she explained, whispering softly into Dieter's ear. 'Cantharides to stimulate, and sweet Eastern spices to prolong your erection and intensify your orgasm.'

Whether it was the effect of the oils, or of Madelon's voice, silky and so full of sex, Dieter's youthful penis soon sprang back to attention; and Madelon knew that her young stallion would still be able to ride her. Her clitoris was throbbing painfully with the desperate desire to be fucked, and she moaned soundlessly as Dieter took her hand from his penis and began his own exploration of her body.

Dieter's tongue played with Madelon's breasts, then ran smoothly down her taut belly and played awhile among the dense undergrowth of her pubic curls. At last, when it seemed that she could bear no more, Madelon felt her lover gently pull apart her cunt-lips and send the tip of his tongue exploring the moist pink world of her cunt.

He toyed a little with her clitoris, and she began to babble incoherently:

'Fuck, fuck, fuck . . . got to fuck . . . Fuck me, my little stallion . . . Stretch my cunt . . . bugger me . . .'

At last she got her wish, for Dieter bade her get on to her hands and knees on the straw, and then

114

mounted her from behind, his wonderfully stiff cock sliding into her like a knife into soft golden butter.

He rode her as nobly as any stallion, squeezing her breasts and toying with her clitty; and they came together, drenching the warm, sweet straw with their mingled love-juices.

They slept for a little while, curled up in each other's arms like little animals. And when they awoke, they fell to fucking once again, as naturally as any two innocent beasts of the field.

Madelon's thoughts drifted briefly back to the present, and she looked round the council chamber with a sigh. Not much here to inspire her; and nothing, certainly, to compare with young Dieter. How virile he was! How strong and hard and smooth his penis had felt, ramming into her cunt, her mouth, her arse!

The old men were still discussing the constitutional crisis. How could they spend so much time on something so boring and essentially trivial? Did it really matter which of the two princes ruled the principality, so long as it had a ruler? Madelon was even becoming doubtful about the attractions of being Crown Princess. After all, the best fucks in Friedenbourg were not necessarily princes . . . She began to wish that Florence Desfarges had won the contest, for all her arrogance and unpleasantness. She at least would have enjoyed her prize . . .

Madelon gazed across the table and realised that the young army officer opposite her was not entirely indifferent to her charms. Moreover, neither was she entirely indifferent to his. He was quite handsome in his uniform really, in a solemn sort of way, and had twinkling brown eyes.

He leaned across the table, and whispered in her ear: 'Are you bored, too?'

She nodded and smiled. 'Shall I entertain you?'

'That is most kind of you, Madelon. You are such a warm-hearted young lady. You really will make an excellent Crown Princess.'

He sat back in his chair, and Madelon wriggled down in hers a little, and kicked off her shoe. She stretched out one silk stocking-clad leg, and stroked the soldier's leg. Instinctively, he realised what she wanted him to do, and his feet slid apart, opening the way for her.

Madelon's toe slid slowly up the officer's calf, then over his knee and up his thigh. She worked her way towards the inside of his thigh, and up still further, until at last she found what she was looking for.

His testicles were firm and juicy to the touch, even through the thick serge of his uniform trousers. She massaged them for a little while, and was gratified to see a little half-smile playing about the corners of the soldier's mouth. Even a soldier's impassivity could sometimes be dented a little . . .

Madelon's foot crept a little higher, and encountered the thick stalk of the soldier's engorged penis. He gave a little gasp as she rubbed it, at first gently, but then with increasing vigour. She could feel it swelling still, even as she rubbed it; and sensed that it would not be difficult to bring his excitement to a peak . . .

Carefully, with infinite patience, Madelon carried out the charming little routine she had practised so many times in lessons at school.

First manoeuvre your foot into exactly the right position . . . feel for the tip of his shaft – yes, that's it. Now, find the topmost button and wriggle your

116

toe underneath it. Now push down, really hard . . . harder. That's it! She felt the thread give way, and the button popped off and fell to the floor with a soft tapping noise. No one seemed to have noticed, so Madelon proceeded to carry out exactly the same procedure for the second and third buttons. The fourth was sewn on so tightly that she despaired of ever achieving success, but at last she found the knack and bravo! she was inside his military breeches.

Underneath, he was wearing standard-issue long pants; but they were gaping open at the front and already his stiffened penis was thrusting obscenely through the gap. It was the work of only seconds for Madelon to tease it through his flies and out into the open air of the council chamber.

She closed her eyes, and explored the soldier's penis with her stockinged foot. Average in length, but thicker than most, it was agreeably hard and a little slippery fluid was already oozing from its tip. She rubbed it cautiously, and was rewarded with a more abundant trickle of juice.

As the old men's voices droned on around her, Madelon amused herself by masturbating the young soldier with her adventurous toes, stroking and squeezing and rubbing at his shaft. Within a few minutes she felt his shaft begin to throb, and moved her foot away from his hardness just in time to avoid being deluged by the outpouring of semen which flooded the front of the soldier's dress trousers.

Far from worrying about what his commanding officer would say when he saw the state of his trousers, the young soldier turned his attentions to his benefactress's pleasure. After all, she had

117

brought him pleasure, so ought he not to do the same for her?

Madelon watched in amazement as – without the slightest regard for those around them – the soldier slid down under the table on to his knees, and began his silent adoration of Madelon.

She sighed with pleasure as she felt the soldier's fingers lifting the hem of her dress and pulling it up above her knees. She felt his warm, moist tongue sliding up the inside of her thigh, teasing the sensitive flesh, awakening the sleeping dragons of her desire . . .

Voices wove a net of fantastical shapes around her as she abandoned herself to the world where only sensation existed. His tongue was on her clitoris now . . .

Two bold fingers were advancing further into her most intimate parts, parting company now – one wriggling into her cunt, the other into her arse. And still that devilishly cunning tongue weaved its sensual spell about her clitoris.

She felt the juices welling up inside her, trickling down onto her thighs, like tears of uncontrollable gratitude. This young, unknown soldier was her saviour, the master utterly of all her desires, of her pleasures and her pain. If he chose to, he could bring her to ecstasy or dash her down into the slough of despond.

He showed her mercy, licking still faster at Madelon's clitoris until at last he felt the silken folds of her vagina and arsehole convulse about his fingers, deluging his tongue with sweet sap.

As the waves of pleasure ebbed away, Madelon heard a distant voice calling to her, calling out her name.

She looked about her, rather bewildered, and realised that all eyes were upon her.

'My dear Madelon,' the Chamberlain was admonishing her. 'Do please try to pay attention. Your devotion to the gentle arts of pleasure is most commendable; but you must learn to take a more active role in matters of state. As Crown Princess-Elect, you already hold a position of great power in the Principality. It is for this reason that we wish to hear your opinions on this matter.'

'What is it that you want to know?' replied Madelon, still somewhat bewildered by pleasure.

'We wish to know simply what you would propose doing to choose which of our princes should be crowned? After all, my dear, whichever is chosen is the man you shall marry.'

'I see . . .' Madelon thought for a moment, smoothing her skirts down over her knees and trying not to notice as the young soldier scrambled back into his seat and tried to cover up the spreading white stain on the front of his dark serge uniform trousers. 'Well, I suppose I should require each of them to undergo trials of sexual prowess. After all, are sexual potency and versatility not regarded as the most valuable of all personal qualities in Friedenbourg? Yes, that is how I should choose the Crown Prince.'

'Bravo, my dear!' cried the elder statesman who had formerly bemoaned the demise of the Imperial era. 'A sensible solution at last!'

And, to Madelon's enormous surprise, the other ministers all agreed with him.

'You yourself shall draw up the list of trials,' declared the Chamberlain, bending to plant respectful kisses on the very tips of Madelon's rosy breasts.

'Now, shall we adjourn for lunch? I have a mind to fuck this rather beautiful and intelligent young lady . . .'

'Oh Alex – it's such a terrible responsibility!' exclaimed Madelon, throwing down her pen and putting her head in her hands. 'I'm not sure I can cope with it.'

'Of course you can, dear Madelon,' scoffed Alex, stroking her breasts soothingly. 'See, you have already thought of the main attributes – strength, beauty, size, endurance . . . all that remains is for us to think of the exact trials. You need a rest. Come to bed, Madelon, and let me soothe you. I am not an expert lover, but I have not yet forgotten all the wise and beautiful things that Signora Delmonico taught us at the Conservatoire.'

Grateful for her friend's wisdom and kindness, Madelon allowed herself to be undressed and led over to the big four-poster with its carvings of nymphs and satyrs, fucking in some fantastical primeval forest.

Alex took Madelon's favourite dildo from the bedside cabinet, and greased it well with sweet oils. She began by sucking Madelon's nipples and then, when she was sure that her friend was relaxed and yet aroused, she parted Madelon's legs and pulled up her knees, revealing the treasure within.

She played a little with Madelon's clitty-ring, marvelling still at the courage Madelon had shown in allowing herself to be pierced in this most intimate of places. Alex had always wanted a clitty-ring, but had been far too shy and afraid of pain to submit to one of the roadside stalls where most Friedenbourgian ladies and gentlemen experienced their first body-piercing. Eventually, Madelon had persuaded her to have one of her nipples pierced, and Alex had to admit that the silver ring she wore through her right nipple had given her great pleasure. But as for her clitty, that was different.

Madelon sighed with obvious pleasure as Alex pushed the dildo into her arsehole, and then took a candle from the bedside table and thrust it into her vagina, filling her up completely. Eyes closed and breathing deeply, Madelon let her mind fill up with images of Dieter, the virile young groom who, despite his lowly birth and station in life, had known instinctively how to pleasure a lady.

As Alex wanked her friend with the dildo and the candle, Madelon remembered the stallion . . . and Dieter, her own little stallion, who had fucked her so beautifully, lulling her into blissful sleep with orgasm after delicious orgasm.

She climaxed with a long sigh of contentment, and then lay panting on the mattress, eyes closed and drifting off into reverie.

'Madelon,' Alex whispered in her ear. 'Madelon – will you do something very special for me?'

Madelon opened her eyes and smiled.

'Of course I will,' she declared. 'You know I'd do anything for you. What is it?'

Alex handed her a sharp needle and a small silver ring.

'Will you pierce my clitty, Madelon?' she begged. 'You're the only person in the whole world I'd trust to do it.'

And as she lay trembling on the bed, waiting for Madelon to push the needle through the throbbing bud of her clitoris, Alex knew that she was about to be ushered, sobbing, into a whole new world of undreamed-of pleasure.

The following morning, Madelon presented her list of trials to the council of ministers, who beamed with delight and congratulated her with the most intimate kisses and caresses.

'Of course, my dear, you will have to be excluded from the trials,' explained the Lord Chancellor, to Madelon's consternation. 'None of the young ladies who took part in the contest can be allowed to take part in the the trials, in case their participation is felt to be prejudicial to the outcome.'

'Then who . . . ?'

'Have no fear, my dear Madelon.' The Chancellor patted the back of her hand reassuringly. 'The trials will be carried out by a number of tutors from the Conservatoire of Delicate Arts: independent experts whose judgement can be trusted utterly.'

So Madelon returned to her bedchamber, wondering what on earth she was going to find to do over the next few days, to help her pass the time. And then she remembered Dieter . . .

'It's going to happen!' squealed Florence, her face a picture of malicious glee. 'You're such a wonderful lover that you're sure to win the trials – especially with *my* help; and then, once you're crowned, you can repeal the law that says you have to marry that stuck-up Madelon. And you can marry me! I'm going to be Crown Princess of Friedenbourg!'

Reinholdt seemed rather less confident of success. He paced the floor of his new Palace apartments uneasily. To tell the truth, he was finding it difficult to come to terms with his newfound royal status.

And the local customs! He had heard tell of Friedenbourg's legendary attitude to sex, of course, but
somehow he had never quite appreciated what a
tremendous effect it must have on the daily lives of
its inhabitants.

He was out of practice! Even living the life of a
notorious libertine had prepared him imperfectly for
the task which awaited him. Would he really be able
to keep pace with his brother Albrecht, schooled in
the arts of pleasure since infancy? And then again,
did he really want to marry Florence Desfarges,
however helpful and obliging she might have been?

Florence interrupted his train of thought, eager as
a puppy to please its master.

'Don't worry, Reinholdt. I'm a pupil at the Conservatoire, remember. I can teach you everything
you need to know to beat the usurper Albrecht at
his own game. And I mean everything.'

She reached up and unfastened the top button of
her diaphanous school blouse, revealing the creamy
swell of her firm young breasts. And, for a little
while at least, Reinholdt forgot all his fears . . .

7   The Confrontation

'No, no, darling: not like that . . . like *this*.' Florence Desfarges was a harsh taskmistress, as Reinholdt was fast discovering.

She knelt astride his face, her clitty poised just too far away, just marginally out of reach of his yearning tongue. That was exactly how she intended it to be.

'Now, Reinholdt. We must stretch your tongue, make it more flexible and versatile. I want you to stretch it just a little bit further, so that it touches my clitty. You do want to taste my clitty, don't you? To taste my juices as they flow from my cunt?'

Reinholdt groaned with desire, and his tongue stretched in a vain attempt to tease the rosebud of Florence's clitoris. Playfully, she moved fractionally further away as the tip of Reinholdt's tongue brushed lightly over her clitty. Just a little further, and he might yet be fit for the trials that awaited him . . .

But Reinholdt was not accustomed to being the helpless plaything of a headstrong girl. In the mountain village where he had grown up, men did not allow their womenfolk to enjoy such power over them. If Reinholdt wanted a girl – and he often did – he simply took her.

He well recalled the first girl he had ever fucked,

when he was hardly more than a boy. Ilse, she was called. Spindly legs, she had, and her face was nothing to write home about, but God, she had huge tits and her cunt was so deliciously tight! He'd ambushed her one warm spring afternoon, when she was bringing her father's goats home from pasture, and simply thrown her down on the grass. He could still recall the scent of wild flowers and the hypnotic buzzing of tiny insects in the air around them as they fucked.

All his life, he had taken any woman he wanted. Perhaps secretly he had known he was not like ordinary men, sensed the royal blood within him? At any rate, he had never taken orders from a woman, and he wasn't going to start now . . .

With a single, swift movement, his strong arms encircled Florence's waist and threw her sideways on to the springy mattress. In an instant he was on top of her, legs astride her firm young torso and his hands pinning her by her arms to the bed.

She looked up at him scornfully.

'Do you really believe that you can take power in Friedenbourg with such foolishness?' Her voice was cold and disdainful, and Reinholdt felt a tinge of unease.

'Listen to me, Reinholdt,' she continued. 'Passion is everything in Friedenbourg. But it must be controlled passion – passion which is ennobled by skill and consideration for the partner. If you persist in this foolish arrogance, you will surely fail in the contest; and you will be sent back to Geneva, to cool your heels. Why, I'm even beginning to wonder if you really are the true prince after all . . .'

'How can you question my royal birth?' demanded Reinholdt.

'If you would be a prince, you must first learn how to act like one.'

Reinholdt glared down at her in angry silence for a few moments; then he sighed, and let go of Florence's wrists.

'Very well. I apologise for my hastiness. Teach me all that you know, and you shall know the strength of my gratitude.'

'There is fire within you, my dear Reinholdt,' smiled Florence, gently stroking the twin globes of his testicles. 'And I shall teach you how to use that fire to defeat the usurper, Albrecht.'

She placed his finger on her clitoris, and began to masturbate him gently. His cock rose in instant obedience, hungry for the taste of her cunt. Good, very good, thought Florence. Tonight, she would teach him all he needed to be a true prince.

The first trial – the trial of Beauty – was to take place in the Great Hall at Castle Amor. When Albrecht and Reinholdt arrived, the ladies of the Conservatoire were already there, waiting for them.

Albrecht blanched a little as he saw that the panel of judges included Signora Delmonico, his father's favourite mistress. She smiled at him as he entered . . . and it was only a smile, yet it struck the chill of fear into his heart. After all, had not Signora Delmonico been with his father when he died? Had her incessant and imaginative sexual demands not contributed to his sudden death?

The other judges were Frau Kässler, art and aesthetics tutor Mademoiselle Julienne, physical education instructress Fräulein Niedermayer, and the Egyptian dancing teacher, known only as Khara.

Each would take special responsibility for certain elements of the trials.

Portraits of the former rulers of Friedenbourg stared solemnly down from the walls of the Great Hall, as though they too understood the significance of this momentous occasion.

The Lord Chamberlain led in the two princes, naked except for loose silk robes veiling their virile attributes. As Crown Prince-Elect, Albrecht wore the royal purple; whilst as a claimant to the throne, Reinholdt wore scarlet.

The two princes took their seats at opposite sides of the hall, and the Chamberlain spoke the opening address.

'Most esteemed ladies of the Conservatoire: you have kindly agreed to lend your expert knowledge and skills to this most onerous state duty. May the nobility of your hearts and the perfection of your art inform your choices, ladies.

'The first trial shall be of beauty, and will take three parts. First, the beauty of the body in repose; second, the beauty of the body during the process of erection; and third, the beauty of the body whilst fucking.'

Reinholdt glanced uneasily around the room. For the first time, he was beginning to realise that what Florence had told him made perfect sense. This was a whole new world of which he knew nothing. How could he hope to defeat Albrecht in a trial of sexual beauty and performance, when Albrecht had been schooled in the art since birth?

Albrecht was brought forward to the dais which had been raised in the middle of the Hall. He climbed the three steps to the dais and unfastened his robe, slipping it off and handing it to the footman

127

who waited beside him. Beneath, he was naked save for the purple amethyst bracelet which proclaimed his identity to the watching judges.

Mademoiselle Julienne came forward and began to explore his body, announcing her findings as she stroked and probed his secret places. She concentrated on his penis, and Albrecht had to muster up all his willpower to prevent his manhood from springing to erection at her touch.

'Not yet, not yet!' he told himself. 'I must show my self-control . . .'

'He has a pleasing body,' announced Mademoiselle Julienne. 'Firm and muscular, and well proportioned. Good, strong thighs and a broad chest.' She ran her fingers down his buttocks and then prised them apart. 'The arsehole is small and aesthetically pleasing.' She tested its firmness with her finger, and nodded appreciatively. 'Tight yet yielding,' she declared.

Then she turned her attentions to Albrecht's penis. As her cool, gentle fingers cradled it like a wounded bird, Albrecht could have wept for desire. But he must not show the strength of his lust! To do so would be to shame his royal birth. And with a supreme effort of control, he succeeded in maintaining his regal composure.

'Ah, yes – a pleasing penis, well-formed and fleshy,' announced Mademoiselle Julienne, palpating Albrecht's prick with delicate and skilful fingers. She ran her fingers down his shaft and cupped each testicle in turn. 'The right is slightly larger and heavier than the other, but both are magnificently formed and full of semen. This is indeed a worthy prince.'

Albrecht returned to his seat, and his place on the dais was taken by Reinholdt, who slipped off his scarlet silk robe and revealed the firm flesh beneath. His flesh was a little less tanned than Albrecht's – for he had spent less time walking naked in the sun – but his body was well muscled and powerful, and drew gasps of appreciation from the watching judges.

Mademoiselle Julienne repeated her minute process of observation, taking out a small jeweller's eyeglass to examine her subject more closely.

'Ah yes, a fine pair of curving buttocks.' She ran the flat of her hand over them appreciatively, and Reinholdt could not stifle a tiny gasp of sensual delight at her delicate touch. Her fingertips' touch was so subtle and skilled and butterfly-soft! But he must remember what Florence had told him . . . don't allow your pleasure to show, not before it is bidden. Don't allow your penis to stiffen, even when your mind is full of the images of rutting beasts, and the irresistible urge to throw that delightful little French girl to the floor, fling up her skirts and take her with all the gusto of a starving man partaking of a good square meal.

Unable to control himself in any other way, Reinholdt clenched his fists, digging his fingernails into his palms until they bit into the flesh and blood began to ooze out. The pain at least blunted the edge of his desire, and he managed to retain his composure until the delectable Mademoiselle had finished examining his arsehole and prick and testicles.

The judges spoke together for a little while, and then the second part of the trial began.

Albrecht breathed a sigh of relief as Mademoiselle Julienne nodded to him. At last he was to be allowed to release the great pent-up tide of his desire. She touched him lightly on the testicles, and immediately the blood surged into Albrecht's penis. Within seconds it had become a great fleshy lance of turgid flesh, a royal rapier, fit to run through any little French girl who might stand in its way . . .

Mademoiselle Julienne ran an expert finger along Albrecht's stiffened shaft.

'A fine example,' she announced. 'It has good proportions, and a pleasing upward curve, with just a drop of sex-fluid at its tip. A good, deep purple . . . and heavy testicles . . . most agreeable.'

To Albrecht's dismay, she left off stroking him and bade him return to his seat, there to wait until Reinholdt had completed the second stage of the trial.

Reinholdt, too, was relieved to be able to relax and allow his desire to inform his prick. Before Mademoiselle Julienne had even touched him, his penis was stiffening in anticipation of her touch. To his surprise, this eagerness was not as well received as he had expected.

'He is a little over-hasty,' remarked Mademoiselle. 'But that is a common fault of youth. We shall see in a later trial how well he can command his libido. As to the general appearance of the cock and balls, I cannot fault them. The skin is smooth and taut, and the head of the penis is of a fine, deep purple hue. The shaft is well lubricated, and the bollocks are balanced and well formed.'

Feeling somewhat uneasy, Reinholdt retired to his seat to await his turn to perform for the judges. Had he perhaps already lost the contest? He felt quite dejected, and wished he had listened more carefully to what Florence had been trying to teach him. If he got through today's stage of the trials, he would be sure to pay more heed to her . . .

A small bed was carried up on to the dais, for the final stage of the first trial. To his surprise, Reinholdt realised that he was being called to perform first.

He didn't have time to feel nervous. By the time he reached the dais, he felt as though he was in a dream. He climbed the steps and sat down on the edge of the bed. Mademoiselle Julienne was getting up from her seat, coming across to him, taking off her white gloves, unbuttoning her dress . . .

Naked save for a diamond necklace and ankle chain, Mademoiselle Julienne lay down on the bed and beckoned to Reinholdt to take her. Now was his chance . . . was he bold enough and skilful enough to take it?

Reinholdt knew that his technique was by no means elegant. His policy had always been to put pleasure first, and forget about aesthetics. But Florence had sounded warning bells in his head, and he knew now that he had to make a special effort. The judges would not be impressed by a prince who fucked like a beast of the field.

Remembering what Florence had shown him, Reinholdt knelt between Mademoiselle Julienne's legs and licked her inner thighs. To his delight, he felt her tremble with pleasure; and he grew bolder, and let his tongue wander into the fragrant and juicy zone between her cunt-lips.

He glanced sideways and saw that the judges were scribbling down notes furiously. Deciding that this must be a good sign, Reinholdt continued to lick out Mademoiselle Julienne's cunt, and was rewarded with an abundant tribute of sweet cunt-juice.

Convinced that his judge was ready for him, Reinholdt thrust into her, rather forgetting his resolution to be elegant in his eagerness to get inside her tight little cunt. He fucked rather jerkily at first, then suddenly remembered that he was being judged not on his skill or speed, but on beauty. With a real effort of will, he managed to moderate the speed of his fucking, entering the Frenchwoman with long, slow strokes. He withdrew with a flourish, as he felt his orgasm coming, and allowed his spunk to fountain out all over Mademoiselle Julienne's creamy-white belly: a very pretty sight.

Reinholdt returned to his seat, unsure as to whether or not he had succeeded in impressing the judges. He could only hope that he had gained in enthusiasm what he had lost in clumsiness. Albrecht approached the dais for the third time, growing in confidence now. Perhaps things were going to go his way, after all. He had little doubt of his own ability to fuck a woman – or a man – and please an audience. Mademoiselle Julienne would not go away disappointed.

His confidence turned to nervousness as he saw not Mademoiselle Julienne but Signora Delmonico getting up out of her seat and walking towards him. She was unfastening the buttons of her silk blouse, and he could see her titties bobbing up and down inside. They were so inviting, and yet he was afraid . . . What if she did to him what she had done to his poor father?

He watched, dry-mouthed, as Signora Delmonico took off her blouse and skirt, revealing honey-coloured nakedness adorned with a pair of white silk stockings and a blue lace garter. She was adorable: truly a dish for a king – or a Crown Prince.

He must try to think straight, try to make himself stop shaking. The judges would be watching his every move, looking to see if he could fuck elegantly.

He knew he could, and yet . . . and yet all of a sudden he felt hopelessly clumsy – far worse than his brother Reinholdt.

She was standing in front of him now, and he knew he must act. His fingers were trembling as he stretched out his arms to her, hardly daring to touch her wonderfully fragrant flesh.

The touch of her breast against his hand was electric, and he started, suddenly brought back to reality. She was smiling at him, a little half-smile that said so clearly: 'Come and get me . . . come and take me. Are you the man your father was?'

The challenge unnerved him. He stood motionless for a moment, uncertain of what to do. His prick tingled expectantly, yet his arms and legs refused to do what his desire demanded. He wanted her, and yet he feared her. But he thought of Madelon, juicy, firm-thighed, big-breasted Madelon; and the thought of her lying in his big soft bed gave him courage. If he failed this test, he would lose Madelon.

He gathered Signora Delmonico up in his arms and laid her down on the bed, gently prising apart her thighs. He felt her relax as his strength overpowered her, and a little sigh of contentment escaped from her lips as he bent to kiss her cunt. It was pink and moist and so, so fragrant.

Albrecht climbed aboard her bountiful body and as they fucked, he felt the grace and ease returning to him. He fucked carefully, mindful of the need to impress the judges; and the slow, easy motion made the touch of Signora Delmonico's cunt feel softer than an angel's kiss about his yearning prick.

As his semen spurted into her, Albrecht knew that, at the last, he had done well. But had he done well enough? It was still so difficult to believe that

133

his crown, his inheritance, his whole life – all were in danger; and that all of these rested upon a few trials of sexual potency. But such were the ways of the people of Friedenbourg; and he must respect the wisdom of their decision.

The ladies of the Conservatoire conferred for a few moments that seemed an eternity, before at last the Lord Chamberlain conveyed their decision to the two princes.

'Your Highnesses, the ladies are agreed. What Albrecht lacks in confidence, he makes up in elegance; whilst Reinholdt's style is rough and untutored, yet it has the naive charm of youthful enthusiasm and vigour. Thus far, we are all decided. Both princes have earned equal merit. We must proceed to the next trial: the trial of form and size.'

Madelon stretched out on the four-poster bed and yawned. The dildos no longer pleased her, and she was even growing weary of Alex's willing fingers and tongue.

'Madelon, dear – is there nothing I can do to help?' pleaded Alex, massaging sweet oils into her schoolfriend's softly curving buttocks.

'Oh Alex, please don't blame yourself,' sighed Madelon. 'It truly isn't your fault that I'm so very bored. You have been the most wonderful of all friends and companions. But you see, I have been too long a student of the Conservatoire to be happy with the company of my schoolfriends alone. I have been educated to provide pleasure to men and women alike, and there, in the giving of sexual pleasure, lies the source of my own delight.'

'Then shall we go out into the town, and find you some suitable partners? There must be hundreds of nice young men in the Garden of Earthly Pleasures who are simply longing to fuck with you.'

Madelon shook her head sadly.

'The Lord Chamberlain has forbidden me to leave the Castle whilst the trials are in progress. If a victor is declared, I must be here to greet him with all the fairest fruits of my body. It's so unfair, Alex – I'm a prisoner here, and yet I have done nothing wrong!'

Alex ran her tongue down Madelon's back and wriggled its moist, pointed tip in between her friend's creamy buttocks. Madelon's arsehole was the prettiest rosebud; she simply longed to kiss it . . .

'I think, Madelon, that there is more to this fit of lassitude than meets the eye,' declared Alex, taking her tongue for a moment out of friend's tight little arsehole. 'Admit it, my sweet: you're missing that little groom who fucked you in the stables!'

'Oh Alex, you're such a mind-reader!' Madelon slid her thighs further apart, so that Alex could toy more easily with her arsehole; and she gave a little shiver of pleasure as she felt Alex's index finger, slippery with cunt-juice, sliding on to the pearly button of her clitoris. In spite of herself, she felt it begin to throb invitingly. 'Yes, yes, I admit it!' she cried, squealing with laughter and delight as Alex tormented her with fingers and tongue. 'If only Dieter were here, I *know* I couldn't be bored . . .'

'No sooner said than done,' declared Alex, giving Madelon's buttocks a last affectionate squeeze. 'You may be confined to barracks, but I'm not.'

And off she went to find Dieter Richtig.

Unfortunately for Alex, she didn't yet know her way around Castle Amor very well. Its rabbit-warren of corridors soon had her quite perplexed, and she wandered up and down them aimlessly for what seemed an eternity before a middle-aged man in royal livery came to her aid.

'Well, well – what have we here?' he hailed her, with a jovial smile.

'I'm afraid I'm lost,' said Alex, rather sheepishly. 'I'm supposed to be on my way to the royal stables, but I think I've wandered rather off course.'

'Never you worry, my dear,' replied her rescuer. 'I'm the Prince's butler – or rather I was. Whether I shall be butler to Albrecht or Reinholdt tomorrow, I haven't the faintest idea – but it's all the same to me. One master is much the same as another. But when it comes to young ladies . . . .' He reached out and stroked Alex's breasts, which were clearly visible through her light summer blouse. 'Tell me, young lady: have you time for a little fucking before I take you to the stables?'

Alex meant to say no – for she was mindful of her duty – but he did have such a wonderful bulge in the front of his uniform trousers . . .

The butler, whose name was Bernhard, took Alex a little way down the corridor, and ushered her politely through a door into a servants' hall, which was where the domestic staff of the Castle took their meals. It was mid-afternoon, and two of the royal gardeners were there, drinking steins of beer, chilled in the castle cellars.

'Good day, Bernhard – what fine filly is that you have there?' hailed one of the gardeners. 'I should dearly love to enjoy her when you have finished with her!'

'Good day, Hans; good day, Olaf,' replied Bernhard, taking off his butler's apron and putting away the silver teapot which he had just finished polishing. 'Well, with the young lady's agreement we can perhaps all enjoy her together. What say you, Alexandra?'

Alex felt quite excited by the prospect of fucking with such rough and ready characters. The butler Bernhard was dressed in his master's costly livery, but was clearly of very ordinary stock – and as for the gardeners, they were obviously peasants, pure and simple. Despite Friedenbourg's relaxed and almost classless attitude to sex, Alex was far more accustomed to the cloistered atmosphere of the Conservatoire, where the tutors and visiting guests tended to belong to the gentler classes. Her clitty began to throb at the thought of rough peasant hands, hard peasant pricks . . .

'I . . . I should be glad to fuck you, one and all,' she replied, as lightheartedly as she could, though her heart was thumping in her chest at the very thought of such an extravagance.

'Then let me assist you out of those clothes, my dear.' The butler's hot, sweaty hands were already easing open her buttons, pulling off her blouse and skirt, revealing her very comely nakedness to the watching gardeners.

Hans got up from the table, faced the wall and took out his prick. As he held his prick and pissed into the drain, Alex saw that the flesh between his fingers was firm and already swelling at the thought of coition with this well-spoken young lady.

Olaf pulled off his boots and took down his breeches. Alex shuddered with delicious fear as she saw how massive his penis was. It was without a doubt the largest she had ever seen – a full nine inches long, and becoming thicker and harder even as she watched.

'Now then, my dear – what would you most enjoy doing?'

Alex blushed.

'Come, come, Alexandra. There's no need to be bashful. We only want to give you pleasure.'

'I . . . I think I should perhaps like to be buggered – and I love to suck cocks.'

'Then kneel down on the floor there, on that rug – that's right, my dear – and let us see what we can do.'

Alex knelt down on hands and knees, her cunt already dripping with the anticipation of this new adventure, and her errand for Madelon almost forgotten. Rough hands ran over her flesh, awakening deep layers of desire she had not even realised existed in her.

Almost before she had had time to enjoy the gentle fingering and smoothing of her naked flesh, she felt a hardness, an unyielding presence pressing up against the flesh of her backside. And Olaf was kneeling before her, thrusting his prick against her lips. Greedy for the strong taste of this unwashed peasant prick, Alex parted her lips and took it into her mouth, very nearly choked by its huge size.

Hans's prick forced her delicate arse with no more delicacy than it would have done the arse of a peasant-woman or some farmyard beast violated for transient pleasure. But Alex's muffled cries were of pleasure, as well as pain. Her education at the Conservatoire had prepared her to accommodate all her lovers' demands, and she thrust back lustily to take in even more of the invading prick.

Olaf was manipulating her breasts, pinching the

nipples as he rammed into her mouth, and causing her such delicious pain that she knew she would come soon, without so much as a fingertip on her clitty.

She looked up and saw that the butler had unbuttoned his trousers and was sitting on the edge of the table, masturbating enthusiastically as he watched Alex and her suitors performing for his own private pleasure.

Never before had Alex known such delight, for her natural shyness had prevented her from often enjoying the wilder sensual delights which were on offer in the parks and gardens of Friedenheim. It was with the profoundest gratitude that she accepted the tribute of two mighty jets of spunk, one in her mouth and one in her arse, joining both with a flood of her own cunt-juice as she climbed to the summit of her own orgasm.

Afterwards, she bade a cheerful farewell to the two gardeners, who doffed their caps respectfully as the butler led her out of the servants' hall and took her out of the castle, towards the royal stables.

Alex found Dieter sitting on an upturned pail in the cobbled stable-yard, chewing pensively on a stalk of grass and looking rather down in the mouth. When he saw Alex approaching, he leapt to his feet and brushed himself down hastily.

'There's no need to look so guilty,' exclaimed Alex. 'I haven't come here to check on your work. In fact, I've come with some news which – to judge from the look on your face – will cheer you up. Madelon wishes you to come to her private apartments. She is missing you terribly . . .'

Dieter's eyes widened in amazement. Could it really be true that he had made such an impression on the future Crown Princess of Friedenbourg? And if so, was he really worthy of such a prestigious liaison? He hardly knew whether to be delighted or terrified.

Alex gave him no time for doubts. 'Hurry,' she said. 'Madelon is waiting.'

And Dieter ran off as bidden, in the direction of the Castle, leaving Alex to wander back slowly on her own.

She would have gone back immediately, but she had just caught sight of *such* a handsome young stable-lad, grooming Madelon's piebald pony. Surely there'd be no harm in staying just a little while longer . . .

Albrecht and Reinholdt glanced at each other nervously. The Castle museum was an unnerving choice as the venue for the second element of the trials, the trial of form and size. But Madelon had fixed on the museum deliberately, knowing that it housed a most intriguing collection of medieval armour, clothing and instruments of love . . .

The late afternoon sunshine filtered in through the arrow-slit windows, casting eerie shadows on the stone floor and patterns of light and shade on the naked bodies of Prince Albrecht and Prince Reinholdt, claimants to the throne of Friedenbourg.

The trial of Beauty had ended in stalemate, and now the judges from the Conservatoire were charged with the task of comparing the dimensions of the two princes' pricks, both erect and in repose. Each judge was blindfolded, and in turn they took the princes' flaccid pricks into their mouths, sucking them to erection and then pronouncing upon the relative merits of their shape, size and consistency.

'Firm, smooth and agreeably sized,' pronounced Frau Kässler, letting Reinholdt's engorged prick escape from her mouth – though she was sorely tempted to suck him to orgasm. But such delights must wait until later trials. 'It has a flowing, upward curve and the testicles are each large enough to fill my mouth.'

'Ah yes,' sighed Khara, her tongue reluctantly leaving the tip of Albrecht's penis. 'But this prick is so thick and strong . . . and so long that it touches the back of my throat easily.'

Since the judgements were again inconclusive, it was determined that the claimants must submit to the medieval artefacts stored in the museum. If their pricks fitted snugly into the iron and leather sheaths and codpieces once worn by Friedenbourg's rulers, and if the love-toys made especially for the von Frieden dynasty were also of the correct dimensions, then they would surely be the true heirs to the principality. If either man's prick proved too small, or misshapen, he would be considered a dishonour to the throne of Friedenbourg.

Reinholdt cried out in a paroxysm of pleasure as Frau Kässler slid his erect penis into the leather sheath, and began to tighten the halter around his bollocks . . .

In her rooms above the Castle Museum, Madelon heard the cries of pleasure from below, and knew exactly what must be happening. Albrecht would be laid out on the bed of pleasure, with the slender iron spike thrusting into his arse and the metal sheath squeezed tight around his thick, hard penis. And Reinholdt would have the leather noose around his balls, pulled tight as the sheath which enclosed his throbbing shaft.

Somehow, Madelon knew that once again, the trial would be indecisive. She had seen and fucked both of the claimants to the throne, and knew that they were equally matched to the point where even she would be unable to choose between them. What would happen if all of the trials ended in a draw . . . ?

But Madelon pushed such thoughts from her mind as there was a timid knock at her bedroom door.

'Is that you, Alex?' She got up and bounded to the door to open it.

Outside stood Dieter, marvelling at her unashamed nakedness. Madelon noticed with approval that his penis was already beginning to swell in joyous anticipation . . .

8 Skill and Endurance

'What on earth is the matter, Dieter?' Madelon took the young groom by the hand and half dragged him into her room. 'You seemed so . . . eager yesterday, when we fucked in the stables. I thought you were as fond of me as I am of you.'

'Oh Madelon!' cried Dieter, his face a picture of agony. 'How could you think for a moment that I am not fond of you? Why, I am fonder of you than of any other living creature. Whenever I see you, my prick leaps up in homage to your glorious beauty, and I long to feel your warm, sweet lips closing about its glistening tip!'

'Then what on earth ails you? If you find me so wonderfully attractive, why do I have to drag you into my bed?' demanded Madelon, much puzzled by Dieter's confusion.

'It is . . . oh, I cannot say! It is . . . that I know I am not worthy of such a liaison – a liaison with the future Crown Princess of Friedenbourg.'

For the umpteenth time that day, Madelon profoundly wished that she had never entered the contest to find a princess for Prince Albrecht. But then again, would she ever have met Dieter if not for the contest?

'Don't be foolish, Dieter,' Madelon admonished

143

him. 'What difference does it make if I am a princess or a pauper? Friedenbourg does not forbid liaisons between any of its citizens – and every princess is allowed to have as many lovers as she chooses! Once I am crowned, we shall still be able to see each other as often as we like. Is that so terrible? Come, Dieter. Let me undress you, and we shall fuck, here, on this silly old four-poster bed. I wish it were a pile of warm, sweet straw, in your stables. But we shall imagine that it is. Here – help me unfasten your tunic. So many buttons!'

Anxious to assuage his fears with the touch of her fingers and lips, Madelon almost tore at the buttons on Dieter's tunic. Perhaps, once they were both naked, the differences between them would not matter any more.

His was a fine, strong body: she would have said a noble body, had she not known that Dieter was nothing but a humble groom who lived with the Prince's horses in the stables. Strong shoulders, broad and muscular; narrow hips and firm thighs, and oh! the most delectable testicles, firm and juicy and inviting. And his youthful penis was already stiff and hungry for her.

She pulled Dieter down on the bed beside her. He made a feeble show of resistance, but Madelon was a prefect of the Conservatoire, and her victory was assured. He allowed himself to sink backwards on to the soft mattress . . .

Madelon set to work on him immediately, anxious not to lose her prize. She straddled him quickly, her gloriously plump backside above his face, and bent to kiss his prick. It was every bit as delightful as she remembered it. The subtle taste of the clear sex-fluid, gathering at the tip of his cock, seemed to refresh Madelon as no other draught of liquid could. It seemed it was welling up from some secret, life-giving spring, deep within his being; and each salty droplet enhanced Madelon's excitement. She stroked and cradled his testicles, handling them with delicacy and gentleness, like wounded creatures which she must restore to life.

And they were responding, quickening, growing firm with life within her grasp. Dieter, maddened with lust, determined to take his sweet revenge. Madelon's creamy-white buttocks were only inches above his face; and within them, the moist pink furrow of her sex. He reached up a trembling hand and touched her firm flesh. Madelon rewarded him with a little sigh of pleasure; and encouraged, he placed his other hand on her hip, and began to draw her down, inexorably, towards his mouth.

Madelon did not struggle or resist. And yet her own pleasure seemed unimportant, compared to the supreme joy of awakening Dieter's youthful lust. His shaft was deep in her throat now, her tongue slippery with the abundant sex-fluid oozing from his prick.

Dieter ran his tongue greedily over Madelon's tempting backside. The flesh was firm and sweet on his tongue, and his head swam with the mingled fragrance of jasmine and awakening sex. Madelon's cunt was beginning to ooze love-juice, and its scent intoxicated him more deeply than any wine. He put out his tongue again, tasting a honey-sweet droplet as it trickled down the inside of her thigh. Heaven. He was assuredly in heaven . . .

Madelon sucked gently at Dieter's prick, teasing him yet refusing to give him release. She wanted him to remember these moments always; remember how wonderful it had felt to be sucked and stroked and aroused by his royal mistress. She could not bear the thought that he might tire of her and leave her.

She gave a deep sigh of pleasure. Dieter's tongue, bolder now, was easing its way between her buttocks; searching out the secret amber rose between the dark furrow of her arse-cheeks. She gasped as its tip darted playfully inside, awakening all her most secret desires. And she sucked a little harder, a little more frantically at Dieter's prick. He cried out – a cry of pleasure that would not be denied, would not be controlled, would not be imprisoned . . .

He came into her mouth, his semen spurting against the back of her throat, warm and thick and salty. And she swallowed it down as Dieter's tongue thrust harder into her arsehole, turning her to a helpless victim of her own pleasure.

Dieter slipped his fingers between Madelon's thighs, and lightly brushed her cunt-lips. The butterfly kiss of his touch on her clitoris brought her to the peak of ecstasy, and she climaxed – silently, speechless with delight, almost fainting away as the cascades of cunt-juice anointed Dieter's upturned face.

Later, when Dieter had fucked her again and again, and brought her to a series of ever more intense orgasms, they lay curled up in each other's arms.

'Madelon,' whispered Dieter, his fingertips idly wandering across her breasts, 'I still don't feel worthy of you. I may be the Prince's favourite groom, but I'm hardly more than a stable-lad, a poor boy from a family of peasant farmers. I'm no match for those high-born courtiers who surround you all day long. And as for you – why, you're the most important and desirable woman in Friedenbourg!'

Madelon laughed, but there was sadness in her heart. How could she ever make Dieter believe that she did not care about his humble birth?

'Oh Dieter, I just know there's something special about you,' she sighed. 'You're special to me, after all, and I am a very discerning judge of character.'

Dieter looked puzzled.

'Special? There's nothing special about me. I'm just like everyone else.'

Madelon giggled, and bent to lick his penis gently and teasingly.

'I bet there's *something* different about you . . .'

Dieter laughed as he remembered his one and only distinguishing feature.

'Well, Madelon, there is one thing about me, one thing that's just a little different.'

'And what's that?'

'Why, Madelon; it's on the tip of your tongue . . .'

Alex strolled through the centre of Friedenheim, revelling in the warm summer sunshine. She felt a little guilty – after all, Madelon was still confined to the Castle, and it must be really awful for her – but it was Alex's afternoon off, and she was tired of being cooped up indoors.

Her adventures with the butler and the groom had given her a newfound confidence in her own desirability. They, at least, had derived pleasure from her company; and oh! what delightful country ways they had of teasing a girl to orgasm. She began to regret all those adolescent years on her father's Suffolk estate, when she had blushed to see the boar mounting the sow, and lowered her eyes discreetly whenever she passed one of her father's estate workers, fucking a plump-tittied dairymaid, or sitting beneath a tree in the cherry orchard, masturbating in the spring sunshine.

Alex had been such a timid child; and now she deeply regretted her shyness. She remembered the time when old Jock, the farm labourer, had taken out his prick and forced her to hold it, feel it swell up between her fingers. He had been so kind to her, and she had spurned him. He had wanted to fuck her and teach her the ways of pleasure, but silly little Alex had been so afraid that she had taken to her heels and run back to the Hall. Her father, Lord Ipswich, had been right to try to persuade her to take a more liberal view of the world. But all his entreaties had been in vain, and sending Alex to the Conservatoire had been a last-ditch attempt to open her eyes to the world of sensual pleasure.

Strange that it had been, not her tutors' classroom teachings but the example of her friend Madelon that had taught her to view the pleasures of the flesh in a new and exciting light. She was so grateful to Madelon. How she wished that all this unpleasantness with the Princes had never happened, and that Madelon was safely crowned Princess of Friedenbourg.

She paused for a moment to look into a shop window, admiring the dazzling array of body jewellery. There was something to suit all tastes and all pockets. Semi-precious stones – garnets, tiger's eye, marcasite – for the prosperous peasant, precious rubies, diamonds and emeralds for the well-to-do of the city, all set into exquisite patterns to adorn the body of the beloved.

There was a set of wedding jewellery in filigree

silver, set with sparkling zirconia: a clitty-ring, two of the sweetest little nipple-rings linked by a delicate silver chain, and even an intricately jewelled dildo for a special wedding gift. For the bridegroom, there was a jewelled silver harness, made to measure to fit tightly around his penis and testicles, and skilfully designed to stimulate his lust and display to his bride the tempting fruits she would soon be tasting.

Alex especially coveted the single sparkling ruby, its golden setting made to be threaded through the pierced flesh of the labia, hanging down tantalisingly between the wearer's thighs. Alex, who had always been so timid, was delighted that she had at last been able to have her clitty pierced. Madelon had always told her the sensations were exquisite, unrivalled, but until now she had never plucked up the courage to face the needle. Perhaps she should now have her labia pierced, too? Her womanhood began to moisten as she thought of the delights of revealing her jewelled cunt-lips to her *amants-de-passage* . . .

A voice behind her made her start.

'Miss Fordham? Miss Alexandra Fordham?'

She swivelled round and found herself looking into a face which she vaguely recognised, but could not quite place. Not a Friedenbourgian, that was for sure. He was far too straitlaced, and seemed a little overawed by his surroundings. She knew she had seen him somewhere recently, though. At Castle Amor . . . ? He had compelling blue eyes, wavy brown hair, a seductive smile, and oh! such a beautiful bulge in the front of his trousers.

'Allow me to introduce myself, ma'am.' The stranger doffed his hat and bent to kiss first her hands, then the tips of her breasts, already pressing firm and insistent against the sheer fabric of her summer blouse. 'Sidney Carter, European Correspondent of the *London Daily Globe*. Your . . . friend Madelon and I have already met; and I saw you in the distance at Castle Amor, the day the trials were announced between Prince Albrecht and Prince Reinholdt. I couldn't help but remember you, Miss Fordham. You have such eminently memorable breasts.'

Alex blushed, and Carter felt suddenly alarmed.

'I hope I have not offended you? I understood that was the accepted form of introduction in this country . . . I'm afraid I'm not very good at this, Miss Fordham.'

Alex laughed, and took Carter's hand in hers.

'My dear Mr Carter, please disregard my blushes, which come not from embarrassment but from pleasure, I assure you. You see, I am so little accustomed to being noticed by men. I am rather shy, as I am sure you can tell – not at all like my Friedenbourgian cousins. Mr Carter, I am extremely flattered that you should find my breasts memorable. And, if I may say so, you seem to have a most interesting penis concealed in those sober serge trousers. May I see it?'

Carter felt as though he were sixteen again, a clumsy boy alone with a girl for the first time, hoping for a quick squeeze of her breasts, wondering how he could keep from spurting into his trousers if she should chance to touch his penis through his trousers . . .

And he recalled that first time, so long ago now, when Dora the housemaid had so comprehensively got the better of him. He'd saved up all his money from his job as a junior messenger at the *Comet* so that he could take Dora out to the music hall, and for a bite to eat afterwards.

He had hoped to steal a kiss from her – maybe even persuade her to let him feel up her tits a bit. But, callow youth that he was, he certainly hadn't expected the barefaced little strumpet to start making up to him in the rear stalls at the Hippodrome! It was when the comic was on – a big, red-faced man who'd had the whole house in stitches with his bawdy tales and comic songs – that Carter had felt a hand on his knee.

It had to be a mistake. It was dark in the theatre. She was feeling for the bag of toffees, and missed . . . But no. There it was again – a very slow, deliberate squeeze of the knee. Why, before Carter had mustered up the courage even to look at Dora, let alone say anything, her fingers had climbed up his thigh, as bold as you please and – good God! There could be no mistake: she was unbuttoning his flies.

He remembered sitting there in stunned silence, staring fixedly at the rubicund face of the comic whilst his own must have been blushing deeper than a boiled beetroot. He thanked his lucky stars no one could see. Please God, don't let anyone turn round and see what she's doing, he'd prayed in silent terror. Don't let anyone see what she's doing, and maybe she'll realise it's madness, and stop.

But a deeper, wickeder voice inside him was praying that she wouldn't stop. Not ever.

Dora's deft fingers were inside his flies now, feeling expertly inside his long-johns for their coveted prize. And now she had him trapped, like helpless prey in the jaws of some marauding beast. And he was terrified. And loving every minute of it.

She pulled him out skilfully, and started wanking him. Good grief! He'd thought she was a timid little virgin, but she wanked him better than he wanked himself, and he counted himself something of an expert. It felt wonderful, wonderful, wonderful . . .

Alas, youth seldom knows self-control; and in a haze of tiny bright lights that seemed to explode inside his brain, Carter spurted forth his youthful tribute. He couldn't suppress a little groan of pleasure, and of course someone in the row in front turned round and saw them – saw him with his prick in Dora's hand, his spunk still dribbling down over her fingers and soiling the front of his Sunday-best blue-serge trousers.

The man just stared at him in silence for a few moments, blinked as though disbelieving the evidence of his own eyes, and then shook his head as though thinking to himself 'Lucky beggar'.

It was the last time he ever saw Dora. She eloped with a fishmonger from Caithness.

And now Carter had that same helpless feeling as he looked at Alex, blushing and soft and feminine and – he was quite sure – utterly ruthless in her passion.

'I'm finding it most . . . educational here in Friedenbourg,' remarked Carter, rather at a loss for something to say. He couldn't stop staring at Alex's breasts, and the inviting dark triangle he could see through the semi-transparent folds of her summer skirt.

'Yes, it's a very different way of life here,' agreed Alex. 'I myself found it quite difficult to adjust to life at the Conservatoire, where sex is considered the most natural and agreeable and noble of all activities.'

'I find you extremely attractive,' said Carter, his throat dry as parchment. 'I should very much enjoy licking out your cunt.'

'I . . . I should very much like to fuck you,' blushed Alex, hardly believing what she could hear herself saying.

'Would you care to accompany me to my hotel?' stammered Carter, hot and cold and wondering why on earth he should feel so confused. Wasn't he a man of the world? A foreign correspondent with an eye for the ladies?

But Alex had really got to him. He looked at the delightful swell of her breasts beneath her diaphanous blouse, and wanted to rip it off her right that second. But he really must control himself. After all, they might be in Friedenbourg, but they were still both English!

Alex astounded him by reading his mind.

'Indeed I should like to spend time with you in your bed,' she replied. 'But that pleasure may be reserved for a later hour. Why should we not fuck here, in the sunshine? As you can see, the citizens of Friedenheim are not bashful about their fucking!'

Carter followed the direction of her gaze, and saw two Polizei engaged in merry fucking with a peasant-woman who was leaning up against the wall, her skirts gathered above her waists, revealing rosy, rounded buttocks. Each was taking his turn with her, and all seemed to be finding the experience agreeable. Across the square, beside the fountain, a group of children were watching, round-eyed with fascination, as an old woman sucked off an adolescent boy. As Carter watched, she took her lips from his tool and gave it a few final strokes with her wrist; and the boy's pearly-white sperm spurted out, forming opalescent droplets on the water.

Slowly, hungrily, Carter reached out and pulled Alex to him. With a single movement he stripped the blouse from her breasts. In seconds her skirt was up around her waist, and his hands were cupping her buttocks, lifting her on strong arms until her thighs were wrapped round his waist and she was high enough for him to ease her deftly on to his upraised penis.

Friedenbourg's ways might be strange, but they had their own special charm.

The Royal Gallery of Erotica had been chosen for the third trial, the trial of skill. Only the judges had been admitted to the gallery, for it was deemed most important that nothing should distract the candidates in their endeavours.

The gallery housed the finest in Friedenbourgian erotic art and sculpture, and few foreigners had ever been admitted to its hallowed precincts: so arousing and unusual were the exhibits that no one untutored in the country's ways could see them and remain unmoved.

Reinholdt gazed around him in stupefaction. Never before had he seen such imaginative displays of sexuality. Statues and portraits depicted in the minutest detail activities which in his adopted country would have been thought culpable and disgusting, if not punishable by death. Already his prick was stirring and he wanted desperately to fuck. But he knew that he must exercise the most extreme self-control. For to spend his powers now would reduce his chances of defeating Albrecht in the trial of skill.

Each candidate was to be allowed one hour with

a judge, during which time he must bring her to orgasm as many times as possible, by whatever means he chose. The judges would assess his prowess in terms of the orgasms he produced in his partner, both in their number and their quality.

The trials were to take place simultaneously, with Albrecht fucking Khara whilst Reinholdt was charged with stimulating Mademoiselle Julienne.

The women stepped forward, naked and ready for the fray. Their determination to withstand all the Princes' advances shone in their faces. For they would not make it easy for the claimants to conquer their resistance . . .

Despite all her good resolutions, Mademoiselle Julienne soon fell prey to Reinholdt's wickedly skilful tongue. Merely by licking and biting at her nipples, he succeeded in bringing her to a first orgasm. As she lay panting at his feet, he began to stimulate her breasts and clitoris together, and within seconds he had brought her to another climax.

Albrecht fared less well with Khara, whose training in Eastern mysticism served her admirably, until he hit upon the splendid idea of stimulating her arsehole with his tongue. Her impassivity fell away like a fragile curtain, and she came once, twice, three times to crashing orgasms which racked her body and left her almost senseless on the floor before him.

Meanwhile, Reinholdt was showing Mademoiselle Julienne how agreeable it is to be buggered whilst having one's nipples and clitoris rubbed. And her cries of ecstasy almost drowned out Khara's groans as Albrecht performed a Tantric ritual which sent her into paroxysms of pleasure.

The judges exchanged meaningful looks. It

seemed pointless to continue the trial. Albrecht and Reinholdt were too evenly matched. Even at this stage, it was obvious that there would be no clear winner.

'My dear Reinholdt, you must take more care of your body,' scolded Florence, rubbing more of the sweet bergamot oil into his shoulders and back. 'See – here are more bites and scratches, and your poor cock is quite bruised and sore.'

'But how can I withstand such ordeals without scars?' protested Reinholdt, wincing a little as Florence massaged oil into his abused prick. 'The demands upon me are too great. I fear I shall not be able to go on.'

Florence put down the oil and sat down on the bed beside him, still massaging his penis with her delicate little hands. It felt so soothing that he forgot the pain, and his apprehensiveness about the next ordeal.

'Listen, Reinholdt,' she breathed, rubbing his penis seductively and knowing that she had his full attention. 'Tomorrow is the most difficult trial yet. It is the trial of endurance. If you fail me in this, you are no man. But I know that you are a man, Reinholdt. Show me that you are a man . . .'

He pulled her face down to his, and kissed her passionately, thrusting his tongue through her lips into the warm moist cavern of her mouth.

She allowed herself to yield, little by little, teasing him and playing him as a skilful angler plays the fish on his hook; until at last Reinholdt had pulled her on top of him and they sank slowly backwards onto the soft mattress, her mouth still crushed against his and the hardening tips of her breasts pressing against his chest. Despite his exhaustion after the day's ordeals, Reinholdt was stiffening. He wanted her, could scent the desire oozing from her cunt; she could feel the tip of his shaft nuzzling against her belly, urgently, yearningly. Such hunger for her; such desire . . . She grew wetter still as she thought of the feel of his firm shaft inside her eager cunny.

Florence lay on top of Reinholdt, still fully clothed although her lover's body was naked. She knew how much it pleased him to enjoy the sensations of raw silk and velvet against his naked flesh; and to tell the truth it pleased her too, to know that she was about to be fucked and possessed by this delectable, naked man, this man who, if she had her way, would very soon be crowned ruler of Friedenbourg.

The mere thought of such power, and of her own association with it, made Florence's cunt grow moister and warmer still. The anticipation of the power that she, too, would enjoy inflamed the throbbing pleasure-centre of her loins. Her clitty was hard, hot, impatient . . .

'Take me . . .' she breathed; and Reinholdt held her still more tightly against him, almost squeezing the breath out of her.

He reached down her back with his right hand, and began ruffling the fabric of her dress, sliding it up gradually in concertina-like folds, which little by little exposed more and more of her beautiful white flesh.

The dress slid up over her backside, revealing that Florence was a true daughter of the Conservatoire – bare-buttocked and ready for love.

'Little slut,' breathed Reinholdt in tones of mock-scandalised delight. 'My sweet little slut . . . You'd sell yourself on a street corner for me, wouldn't you?

You'd fuck with the filthiest vagabonds or the beasts of the field if you thought it would please me. And what pleases me most is that you would take delight in the filthiest obscenity, the vilest perversion. You are a true daughter of Friedenbourg, my sweet little harlot . . .'

Charmed by Florence's shamelessness, he began to stroke the flesh of her backside. Gradually, her legs slid open and her buttocks began to part, revealing the bounty within. With a grunt of triumph, Reinholdt slid his index finger between Florence's arse-cheeks and sought out her tight little arsehole. She squealed with irrepressible delight as his finger-tip pressed playfully against the gate to her secret garden – the lightest, slightest pressure; and yet her intimacy opened up like a flower and welcomed him in. In one swift movement, his finger disappeared inside her, swallowed up and engulfed by her willing flesh.

Enraptured by Reinholdt's boldness, Florence felt her cunt turning into a river of desire.

'Oh fuck me, fuck me,' she groaned. 'I would do anything for you, my prince . . . ! Bind me, beat me, drag me through the streets bruised and naked and filthy with semen and blood . . . make me your willing slave . . . only fuck me, fuck me my darling prince!'

With his free hand, Reinholdt tugged at Florence's skirt, pulling it up at the front so that her thighs and belly were completely naked and pressed up against him. Her pubis rubbed against Reinholdt's hardness, and little droplets of clear sex-juice brushed off on to her blonde curls, sparkling like exotic, fragrant dewdrops.

His finger still firmly inside Florence's arsehole,

Reinholdt put his free hand underneath the swell of her buttocks and eased her up his body until her cunt was just at the right level for him to ease her on to the tip of his penis. And how could she refuse or resist? Already her legs were straddling him and her cunt was yawning wide for him.

His prick slid into her suddenly, and she felt its hardness thrusting savagely against the neck of her womb. His eagerness caused her pain, and yet she was enjoying greater pleasure than she had yet known – eager pupil though she had proved. Such delicious hardness . . . She answered him with strong thrusts of her pelvis, and together they rode to the summit of ecstasy.

Although half-dazed with pleasure, Florence had not forgotten her duty to bring Reinholdt delight, too. Squeezing her cunt-walls subtly around his penis, Florence almost forced the love-juice from Reinholdt's loins; and the hot white spurt of his semen was the signal for her, too, to cry out in the throes of ecstasy.

As they lay together on Reinholdt's bed, idly stroking each other's naked bodies, Reinholdt turned to Florence with a smile.

'So – you have discovered that it is to be a trial of endurance tomorrow? Why should I fear such a thing as that? Have I not, these long nights, fucked you from dusk till dawn, and only given pause because you begged me to show mercy?'

Florence shook her head.

'You don't understand,' she replied. 'The trial is one of endurance, not of stamina. The judges know that you can fuck all night long and not grow weary. What they want to know, my darling, is this: can you withstand extremes of pleasure . . . and of pain?'

Seeing Reinholdt's expression turn from confidence to unease, Florence slid off the bed and opened the little leather case she had brought with her. Inside were strange and baffling objects – a velvet glove, trimmed with fur; another, its leather palm studded with cruel spikes; straps and harnesses and implements with sharp, sharp spikes; a wafer-thin blade of the finest surgical steel . . .

'Time is short,' said Florence, taking one of the gloves from the case. 'And you have much to learn. But submit to me, my darling, and I shall make you master of the trial . . .'

In the dungeons beneath Castle Amor, where Madelon had so lately undergone torments at the hands of the Executioner, the two claimants to the throne of Friedenbourg waited nervously to learn what would be the substance of this, their fourth trial.

The invited onlookers, sworn to absolute silence lest they disturb the course of the trial, sat in dark alcoves, hardly daring to breathe, as the Lord Chamberlain stepped forward.

'Your Highnesses,' he announced, 'the fourth trial is a trial of endurance, and it will be a worthy Prince who steps forth from it as the victor. Lots have already been drawn, and Prince Albrecht shall be first to take his turn. Prince Reinholdt shall be taken from this chamber, and shall wait until he is summoned to answer to his judges.'

Reinholdt was led off into a neighbouring dungeon, where he was bound and blindfolded. Silence wove a net of unreality about him; the only sound, the insistent drip, drip, drip of water from the cold, slimy walls, hewn from the rocky hillside on which

Schloss Amor stood. The time passed so slowly there, in the darkness, that it seemed an eternity. He became disorientated. He thought that he heard . . . something; something indistinct and very far away.

Could he hear faint cries of pain . . . or were they of pleasure? At last, two of the Palace Guard came to collect him, and led him back into the main dungeon chamber, where his blindfold was removed. He blinked in the candlelight, just in time to catch a glimpse of Albrecht, leaning heavily on the arms of two guards as he was led out of the chamber.

Reinholdt told himself that he was not afraid. After all, hadn't Florence prepared him well for his ordeal? The ordeal had obviously weakened Albrecht: surely he, Reinholdt, the true Prince of Friedenbourg, could do better?

Nevertheless, his heart sank as he looked up and saw a tall, massively built figure coming towards him: a masked man, powerfully muscled and naked save for a studded leather belt and apron, and heavy boots. A long-handled whip was stuck through his belt.

Reinholdt knew him at once. It was the Executioner: a man whose face had never been seen. A man whose trade was death. A man trained to inflict a hundred different degrees of pain – precisely and efficiently.

'Stand against the wall, and place your hands and feet into the shackles,' commanded the Executioner. 'The first ordeal shall be of pleasure.'

Reinholdt obeyed, his mouth dry and his palms sweating with anticipation. What strange pleasure could involve being shackled to the wall of a dank and dismal dungeon?

The iron shackles snapped shut about Reinholdt's

wrists and ankles, and the Executioner spoke again. His voice was polite, yet full of menace.

'You shall be blindfolded once again,' he announced, 'and your body shall be subjected to a number of pleasurable sensations. You must not, under any circumstances, respond to the pleasure. If you show any response, you shall be deemed to have failed the trial.'

Reinholdt submitted to the blindfold, and was plunged once more into darkness.

And the ordeal began.

Strange and wonderful sensations assailed him in the void of his darkness and confusion. Some he could identify without difficulty – the rich smoothness of velvet, sliding across his testicles; the secret pleasure of a tongue, curling about his nipples – but others were arcane, mysterious, terrifying in the pleasure they provoked. Others were so acutely, intensely pleasurable that the pleasure almost became pain . . .

Was that honey, being dripped from a cool silver spoon on to his prick? And now the agony of pleasure as something sharp and rasping ran over the tip of his glans. Stop, stop! He could not bear it. He must not respond! What was that exquisite sensation rippling through him as something firm yet yielding slipped into the secret chamber of his arse?

Beads of sweat were glistening on his brow, trickling down his face. He could taste the salty liquid on his lips. But he knew that he was stronger than the pleasure; he could defeat it. Resolutely, he refused to respond. His penis yearned to spring to attention, but he resisted. He was going to succeed! Albrecht would be defeated, and Reinholdt would become Crown Prince of Friedenbourg!

162

He hung, exhausted, from his manacles; so weak that he hardly noticed as the Executioner unlocked his chains and two strong guards helped him to walk slowly across the chamber.

'Lay him on the rack, and tie him securely,' commanded the Executioner. 'The second part of the trial will take the form of an ordeal of pain. Pain to which you must not respond in any way . . .'

A frisson of fear ran through Reinholdt. He did not fear pain, and yet . . . What terrible form might it take? What if he could not withstand it? Were they going to break his body on the rack?

He submitted to the guards, who laid him on the wooden bench and tied his wrists to the spindle of the rack. Leather straps about his waist secured his torso. But, instead of tying his feet to the bottom rail of the rack, he was surprised to find his legs drawn up at the knees and secured, wide apart, revealing the secrets of his nakedness to all who cared to see. What horrors did the Executioner intend to perpetrate upon him?

The first part of the ordeal, he withstood with ease: long, steel pins, wickedly sharp, pushed through his nipples and scrotum. That part was easy to bear, for Reinholdt had had his body pierced many times. He scarcely flinched as the fine steel blade ran over his scrotum, making beads of blood stand out upon the puckered surface. Nor did the whip give him any cause for fears, even when the Executioner thrust its long wooden handle up into his arse, masturbating him with it. He would not respond. He would betray neither pain nor pleasure . . .

Alas, Reinholdt was not so well prepared for the last part of the trial. Silent and impassive, the

Executioner removed his leather apron, revealing his massively swollen penis, clad in a studded leather sheath. Reinholdt's eyes widened in alarm as he saw the spikes adorning the sheath, long and hard and unyielding. Surely he was not going to . . . ?

He bit his lip and stifled a cry of pain as the Executioner knelt between his thighs and without warning thrust his spike-clad penis into Reinholdt's arsehole. It felt as though he was on fire, being torn apart by a monster with iron claws. And worse, far worse than the pain, was the pleasure, the terrible unremitting pleasure that the pain itself was bringing him.

He wept openly as his prick rose to attention and, after only a few strokes of the Executioner's prick, spat forth its venom on to his belly. The ecstasy of his orgasm soon gave way to shame and bitter grief. He had been defeated. He had lost the trial.

It was not until Florence had helped him to a seat that he realised he had been mistaken.

'Albrecht failed the trial, too,' she exclaimed. 'He was no more able than you were to withstand the trial of pain. You still have one more trial in which to prove your worth; and I am going to make sure that you succeed.'

'I'm sure we shouldn't be doing this.' Dieter helped Madelon to climb out of the window and down the ladder which he had brought from the stables. 'Haven't you been commanded to remain in your apartments until the trials are over?'

'But Dieter, it's such a beautiful day, and I just can't bear being cooped up inside any longer.' Madelon caressed his prick through his corduroy breeches, and felt his resistance melting away. 'I know it's a dreadful thing to do, defying the Lord Chamberlain's orders, but really I can't see what harm we're doing, just by going for a ride in the forest. We shall be back by lunchtime, long before anyone has noticed that I've gone.'

Luckily there was no one about, so they were able to reach the stables without drawing attention to themselves. Dieter saddled Madelon's piebald pony, and took a chestnut gelding for himself, and they rode off swiftly, down the slopes of the mountain and into the forest which covered much of Friedenbourg.

They spent an hour or so just chasing each other merrily in and out of the trees on horseback, and then, weary of the game, found a secluded clearing beside a sparkling stream, and lay down on the grass to enjoy subtler pursuits.

Madelon tugged at Dieter's buttons, anxious to free his prick so that she could suck it and taste the wonderful salty semen on her tongue.

'Oh Dieter,' she sighed, running her tongue along the underside of his shaft, 'you are such a fine rider – a natural horseman. Won't you ride me now, and show me how you master a little wild mare?'

Laughing, Dieter flung her to the ground and tore off her skirt, leaving her quite bare from the waist down, save for the glittering diamond hanging temptingly from the lips of her cunt.

'On your knees, filly!' he cried. 'I am going to ride you, whether you wish it or not!'

He hauled her up on to her hands and knees, and gave her bare rump a few playful slaps which reddened her buttocks most delightfully.

'To horse!' cried Dieter, and, pulling apart Madelon's arse-cheeks, he was soon in the saddle, his fine fat cock impaling her moist, rosy cunt.

Madelon thrust out her backside; and reaching back with one hand between her legs, she succeeded in cradling Dieter's testicles in her palm. Giving them a gentle squeeze, she brought him to his first orgasm, and he plunged deep into her, clasping her arse-cheeks as his semen flooded her cunt.

'Now I shall be the horseman!' exclaimed Madelon, rolling Dieter on to his back and masturbating him into renewed stiffness – a task which took only moments, for he was very youthful and vigorous. Then she slid her cunt, still dripping with his semen, over his cock, not riding him side-saddle, like some old-fashioned lady, but straddling him bareback, like the finest horsewoman in Friedenbourg.

They were deep in pleasure when they heard the voices, at first faint, but getting gradually nearer with every moment.

'Madelon! My lady Madelon! Where are you . . . ?'

'The servants!' exclaimed Madelon. 'They must have noticed that I was gone, and now they have come after me! Oh Dieter, forgive me: I have dragged you into this, and now we are both going to suffer for my foolishness.'

Dieter was protesting that he was just as much to blame when the sound of horses' hooves announced the arrival of the search party.

9   The Trial of Taste

The party of three horsemen rode into the clearing, with a clatter of harness and a pounding of hooves. Madelon caught sight of their scarlet jackets through the trees. Soldiers from the castle guard!

There was no question of escape, nor any hope that they might mistake what Madelon and Dieter were doing; for Madelon was still bare-buttocked and astride her surrogate steed, his semen running out of her cünt and trickling down on to his bare belly.

Madelon recognised the soldiers at once: they were three of the guard responsible directly to the Lord Chancellor, and whose job was to act as personal bodyguards to members of the Royal household. They were strong men, skilled in arms and accustomed to the heat of battle. Lusty men, too; for it was said that they took their pleasure every bit as seriously as they took their military training . . .

Their leader, a tall, broad-shouldered fellow by the name of Tarnheim, had wanted to fuck Madelon in the Garden of Earthly Delights one spring afternoon when the young ladies of the Conservatoire had been taken there by their tutors for an educational visit. Alas, Madelon had been forced to refuse, for she and her classmates had to hurry away to see a demonstration of arse-fucking. She could still recall the regret with which she had turned away the Captain, and the thundercloud of angry disappointment which had passed across his face. He was evidently a man who was unaccustomed to having his wishes denied.

And even now, Madelon wished that she had slippèd away from her classmates and let him fuck her. She was sure it would have been an agreeable experience for both of them. She wondered if, just by chance, Captain Tarnheim remembered her and still wanted to fuck her. Might he be amenable to a little gentle persuasion? And yet, he looked so very stern, so stony-faced . . .

The Captain dismounted from his mare and tethered her to a nearby birch tree.

'My lady Madelon,' he thundered. 'How could you dare to disobey the express wishes of the Lord Chancellor? How dare you neglect your royal duties for the paltry favours of this . . . this stable-lad?'

Dieter sprang to his feet and stood before Madelon, desperate to protect her from the invaders.

'I am the Prince's head groom!' he cried. 'I am no stable-lad! And if I were, I should be no less proud to serve his Royal Highness and the lady Madelon. Give me a sword, so that I may defend my honour!'

But Madelon gently pushed him aside and stepped forward.

'Dieter is young, and as fiery in questions of honour as he is in the ways of love. I . . . we meant no harm. I was so bored and lonely all alone in my apartments. Can't you understand that? I know it was wrong, but . . . I am just a warm-blooded young girl, barely more than a child. Responsibility hangs heavy upon my girlish shoulders.'

She smiled at Captain Tarnheim, making sure that he appreciated the generous swell of her exuberant breasts. 'I so longed to leave the stuffy castle and come out here, into the fresh air. It is such a beautiful day, and my lord Albrecht is so preoccupied with the trials that he no longer has the time to come and fuck me. My cunt was aching for a good fucking. It aches still . . .'

'That may be so,' replied the Captain, fighting back emotions which threatened to overwhelm him. 'But surely you can see that you ought not to have allowed yourself to be led astray by this young fellow – and him no more than a lowly stable-lad, for all his arrogance! Why, there will be ample time for such as he when you are crowned. Your largesse towards the poor of Friedenbourg will do you credit. But for now, allow me to teach this young puppy a lesson . . .'

With a cruel smile, he drew his cutlass and advanced towards Dieter, who, deprived of any weapon with which to defend himself, was forced back, in fear of his life. But he refused to turn tail and flee. Backed up against a tree, Dieter glared back murderously as Tarnheim pressed the sword-point against the groom's helpless throat.

'No, no!' cried Madelon. 'Dieter is not at fault in this! Spare him, I pray of you. He mustn't take the blame for my weakness! It was I who led him astray . . .'

She acted swiftly, unfastening the buttons of her blouse and baring her magnificent firm breasts, peeling back the fabric, sliding the silky blouse off her shoulders and letting it fall to the forest floor. The large pink nipples grew stiff and welcoming as the early summer breeze played over her delectable flesh. Naked, she stood in the middle of the clearing, Dieter's semen sticky and fragrant on her strong, smooth thighs.

'Won't you punish me, instead, Captain?' She walked across to where Captain Tarnheim stood, and knelt at his feet on the soft fragrant grass, dappled by the mellow sunlight that filtered through the canopy of leaves. She reached up and caught hold of Tarnheim's sword-arm, pulling it gently but firmly downwards until the blade was within reach of her lips.

Madelon kissed the point of the sword, and ran her fingers and tongue up the flat of the blade, as though caressing a lover's penis.

Tarnheim could not remain unmoved by such an open display of willingness and desire. He sheathed his sword, unbuckled his sword-belt, and let it fall to the grass; then he unfastened the top button of his uniform trousers. Madelon took her cue instantly, and quickly unfastened the rest of the buttons. Underneath, the Captain wore coarse linen pants. Madelon reached inside, and her cool fingers encountered firm, warm, eager flesh, pulsating with blood.

'I want you . . .' she breathed, pulling out the Captain's stiffening penis. 'I want to suck your beautiful cock, and lick your balls and enjoy the taste of your semen on my tongue. I want you to violate and use and humiliate me, here on the forest floor, in front of your men. And then I want you to give me to your men as a plaything. I want you to do anything and everything with me. I will not disappoint you. I promise you that . . . Only, I beg of you – show us leniency.'

Dieter watched in jealous despair as Madelon began to lick the Captain's balls, the touch of her long and muscular tongue causing the scrotum to tense in eager anticipation of emission. She had such a beautiful tongue – long and moist and pink. How often it had twisted around the tip of Dieter's penis. His cock rose in sympathy with the scene.

The Captain put his fingers into Madelon's mouth, and forced it open wider. There was no need to force her – she would willingly have swallowed down his prick – but he needed to feel the power of his ascendancy over her. Quickly and brutally, he forced his cock between Madelon's rosy lips; and she heard him sigh, almost inaudibly, as his prick disappeared from view.

Madelon worked away with a will. She must not displease the Captain, for if he betrayed her to the Lord Chancellor, what terrible punishments he might decree for her disobedience! Her expert fingers caressed Tarnheim's bollocks, teasing him to bursting point. A few more gentle licks of her tongue, and he would be there.

But Tarnheim had other plans for her. It was too easy, letting himself come in her mouth. And she was altogether too willing. What sort of punishment was this? Why not make her suffer a little before showing her mercy? Why not enhance his own delight by causing the little filly some pain? She had begged him to abuse her: why then, he would not demur . . .

The Captain pulled his penis from Madelon's lips, smiling sardonically at the look of surprise on her

face. He left her kneeling on the grass whilst he
foraged in his saddle-bags for a couple of stout ropes.

'Leave her alone! Don't you dare harm her!' cried
Dieter, struggling to escape from the two guards
who held him fast. But they merely threw him to
the ground, the points of their swords against his
chest; and he was forced to watch the rest of the
spectacle in horrified silence.

Tarnheim pulled Madelon to her feet, and dragged
her across the clearing towards a small stand of birch
trees. Taking the ropes from his belt, he tied her
securely between two trees, one arm secured to each
of two sturdy trunks. She struggled a little, as yet
unafraid, but aware that this display of fear was what
would most please Tarnheim. Like most beasts of
prey, he preferred his victims to be alive and
kicking . . .

Tarnheim stepped up behind her, his sword once
more in his hand. He stood in silence for a moment,
and all Madelon could hear was his frantic breathing
as he masturbated himself in contemplation of her
delicious backside. Madelon anticipated the blow,
but when it came it was more vicious even than she
had expected. The flat of the sword-blade swished
down upon her buttocks like the bite of a thousand
vipers, and she strained against her bonds in an
involuntary spasm of pain.

Again and again and again, the blade bit into her
back and buttocks, and she felt as though her flesh
were on fire, incandescent with the white-heat of
pain that is both horrifying and delicious. The insidious warmth of lust began to mingle with the pain,
making her babble deliriously . . .

'Oh yes, punish me, punish me, beat me, fuck me,
fuck me . . . I am unworthy, I am nothing before

172

the power of your fire . . . oh fuck me and burn my sins away . . .'

Tarnheim continued beating her with the flat of his sword, his face registering only impassivity, but his prick dripping with the honeydew of lust.

Throwing down the sword, Tarnheim began to gather up the many dried birch-twigs which littered the forest floor. Madelon watched, baffled, as he collected them into a bundle and then took up his position behind her once again.

The assault upon the delicate flesh of her arse was almost more than Madelon could bear. One by one, she felt arrows of pain searing her body as Tarnheim thrust the sharp twigs into her arse. One, two, six, eight . . . Madelon lost count, lost in the delirium of mingled pleasure and pain. Surely her arsehole would split! She could feel the flesh stretching, stretching, tearing . . . Was that a drop of warm blood, trickling down the inside of her thigh . . . ? She cried out again and again, but Tarnheim showed her no mercy.

When Madelon could take no more, and hung, close to unconsciousness, from the ropes which held her fast to the trees, Tarnheim at last gave way to the urges which tormented him; and, wrenching apart her reddened arse-cheeks, he gazed with delight upon her little brown arsehole. In a single sword-thrust his penis was inside her, and she was howling once again with the pain and pleasure of her mortified, martyred flesh.

Madelon raised her tear-clouded eyes and saw that the two soldiers had also unfastened their flies and were masturbating as their Captain buggered his priceless prisoner. The sight of their hands on their hardened shafts only served to intensify Madelon's perverse and unwilling delight, and she came to a juddering orgasm whose shock-waves triggered off the Captain's fountaining semen.

Sated at the sweet spring of Madelon's loins, the Captain wiped his prick and turned to his men.

'You may do with her as you wish,' he instructed. 'But do not harm her, for she must afterwards be returned to her apartments at the Castle. No one must know that she ever left.'

Seeing Madelon's look of gratitude, he turned to Dieter.

'You, boy, have presumed too much upon your lover's goodwill. For your punishment, you shall be whipped and sodomised by my men until they have sated themselves on your body, after which, you are free to return to Castle Amor. The lady Madelon's generous heart has spared you further torments.'

The forest resounded to Madelon's cries as the soldiers slaked their lust upon her sweet and tender flesh.

Madelon returned late to her apartments, bruised and sore yet strangely elated. Dieter was safe, and Captain Tarnheim had given his solemn undertaking that no one would ever hear of Madelon's disobedience. Though cruel in his pursuit of pleasure, the Captain was certainly a very handsome man . . .

As she opened the outer door of her apartments, Madelon heard curious sounds coming from her bedroom. Was there an intruder? If Alex was in there, she was certainly not alone . . . Silently, she crept towards the bedroom door, and knelt down to peer through the keyhole.

Alex was indeed inside Madelon's bedroom – and as Madelon's lady-in-waiting, she had every right to be. But Alex was not alone, and nor was she attending to her official duties. She was lying naked on the bed which she and Madelon had so often shared, her dainty knees drawn up and her pretty little brown-fringed quim clearly visible between her slender white thighs.

Beside her knelt a tall young man with a shock of chestnut-brown hair. Although he was facing away from her, Madelon recognised him at once as Sidney Carter, Foreign Correspondent of the *London Daily Globe*. Well, well, she thought, so this is how timid little Alex spends her leisure hours. Perhaps my sisterly words of advice were not all in vain, after all.

As Madelon peered through the keyhole, she saw Carter take a small wooden box from the bedside cabinet, open it and remove a pretty dildo, made from polished ebony. It had been a gift from Alex's father to his daughter, when Alex first came to the Conservatoire; and Madelon smiled as she remembered the many times the two girls had put it to good use in the dormitory.

Carter bent to kiss Alex's cunt, and Madelon heard her sigh softly. Then he delicately slid the dildo into Alex's arse, and began to wank it in and out of her, still bending to tongue her clitoris.

Alex began to babble incoherently – not words, but wordless sounds of mounting ecstasy, of pleasure that will not be denied, and which is so intense that it robs its victim of the power of speech.

With a loud groan of pleasure, Alex fell back on to the bed; and Madelon could see a clear honeydew trickling slowly out of her cunt, on to the embroidered coverlet. How well Madelon recalled the taste of that clear, sweet, priceless fluid! Its sweetness was on her tongue even now . . .

Within seconds, Carter was on top of Alex, fucking her for all he was worth, the ebony dildo still protruding from her arse. Madelon shivered with vicarious pleasure as she thought how wonderful it must feel.

The two lovers made a handsome pair as they climaxed together, and sank back on to the bed, breathing heavily.

Madelon saw that this was her cue to enter; and she made great play of having only just arrived. With a pantomime of noise and ceremony, she entered the bedroom. Alex and Carter had just enough time to tidy themselves up a little, and Madelon found them sitting side by side, quite naked, on the bed. The room was filled with the unmistakable aroma of sex – of sugar-sweet fanny-juice and fresh spunk.

Alex looked up rather guiltily as Madelon came in.

'I . . . we're sorry. I hope you don't mind . . .'

Madelon laughed.

'Mind? My dear Alex, I rather hoped you two might stage a little encore for me. I have had quite a trying afternoon with Captain Tarnheim and his men, and I should dearly love to witness a good fucking. Or better still, take part in one: I'm sure it would refresh my spirits . . .'

'Please forgive my being so inhospitable,' interjected Carter. 'My behaviour really is unpardonable. I haven't yet quite accustomed myself to the customs of this charming country, though your friend Alexandra is doing an admirable job of converting me. Won't you join us in bed? I for one should most certainly enjoy the honour and pleasure of fucking you once again . . .'

'How gracious of you,' exclaimed Madelon, hastily

discarding blouse and skirt and shoes and reducing herself once more to the blissful state of nakedness.

'Oh Madelon! What has happened to you?' Alex ran soothing fingers over her friend's bruised and lacerated backside. 'You're hurt!'

Madelon smiled and patted Alex's hand.

'It was all in a good cause,' she replied cheerily. 'And it was not entirely without its pleasurable aspects . . . though poor Dieter suffered a little at the hands of those rough soldiers.'

Carter and Alex made room for her, and she lay down on the bed between them, wincing a little as her bruised back rubbed against the embroidered coverlet.

'Lie on your belly,' instructed Alex. 'And I shall soothe your wounds. Do you remember the time Herr Göttingen whipped us because we made fun of his little tiny cock? We couldn't fuck for days! Now, lie down and let me get to work.'

Madelon laughed and obeyed, stretching out on the coverlet and luxuriating in the light summer breeze filtering through the curtains and playing across her flesh. Alex reached into the drawer of the bedside cabinet, and took out a little porcelain jar of ointment – a decoction of soothing oils and sweet herbs, made up to a secret recipe known only to the Matron of the Conservatoire. This ointment was used frequently by the junior girls, to ease the hurts caused by over-zealous fucking, or by tutors and lovers whose tastes lay more in inflicting pain than in sharing pleasure.

Alex handed the jar to Carter, who sniffed it appreciatively.

'Strong stuff,' he commented, dabbing his finger into the jar and taking out a little ointment. As he put his finger to his nose and smelt the sweet vapours, his head spun with the sudden inhalation of powerful aphrodisiacs; and his prick began to return to its former state of readiness. 'Wonderful stuff: what is in it?'

Alex shook her head and smiled.

'It's a trade secret, I'm afraid. Even Madelon and I don't know, for Matron guards her recipes jealously! Now, my dear Mr Carter, if you wouldn't mind just holding the jar for me whilst I massage some of the ointment into Madelon's back and buttocks . . . ? Or perhaps you would like to help?'

Madelon gave a little sigh of contentment as Alex's fingertips smoothed the cooling ointment into her burning flesh. She began at the shoulders and worked her way down, Carter lending his aid by running his greedy tongue over each inch of Madelon's flesh that he could reach. Of course, such was the strength of the herbs in the ointment that they could easily be absorbed through the skin or tongue; and as Alex and Carter anointed Madelon's flesh, they too received the soothing and stimulating benefits of the aphrodisiacs . . .

Carter groaned with desire as he watched Alex's nipples stiffening and his cock rearing its head in insistent lust.

'I want you,' he gasped. 'I . . . I want you both. Now! I must have you both now!'

'Time enough, time enough,' replied Alex, in greater control of her desires, yet still panting with lust.

Her fingers ran expertly over Madelon's lower back, and then delved lower, into the secret amber furrow between her buttocks. Traces of Captain Tarnheim's semen still oozed from her arsehole, and

Alex lovingly licked away the sticky white fluid, before gently inserting her fingertip through the secret gate, laden with the soothing and exciting cream.

Madelon twisted and turned in an agony of pleasure as Alex's finger explored the inside of her arse, spreading the aphrodisiac ointment along the walls, stretching and testing and titillating them.

'Oh bugger me, bugger me!' cried Madelon, unable to control herself any longer. Carter, ever the English gentleman, was quite unable to restrain himself. Already his cock was near to bursting point, and the sight of Alex's finger up Madelon's arse was the last straw. He handed Alex the ebony dildo, liberally smeared with the ointment, and watched hungrily as Alex thrust it up Madelon's backside. Then, as Alex knelt between Madelon's thighs, buggering her with the dildo, he knelt behind her and, smearing his already incandescent cock with the aphrodisiac cream, pulled apart Alex's arse-cheeks.

Alex had a delightful arse, very small and very tight, for she had never been buggered until her uncle gave her to the drunken footman on her sixteenth birthday; and because of her shyness, Alex had not attended to her lessons at the Conservatoire quite as conscientiously as her fellow pupils. As a consequence, her arse had never been properly stretched, and she still found it quite difficult and sometimes painful to accommodate even a modest-sized prick. Carter's was thick and long, and its tip was even now forcing its way into her backside.

'Ah! No! Mercy!' cried Alex; but there was lust in her cries of protest, for the aphrodisiac ointment had done its work well.

Carter paid no heed to Alex's protests, and continued to thrust home. She was so tight that he feared he might tear her delicate flesh, but luckily the cream eased his way a little, and the perineum stretched slowly to accommodate him. Once inside her forbidden temple, the tightness felt exquisite, like a firm hand around the base of his prick, or perhaps the eager lips of some expert fellatrice . . .

Madelon spent copiously, her clitoris titillated to orgasm by the roughness of the embroidered coverlet on which she was lying. Maddened with lust, Alex left off wanking her with the dildo, and concentrated on thrusting backwards, clenching her buttocks in an attempt to give Carter even greater pleasure.

She felt his hand move down her belly, towards her pubic curls. Now he was feeling . . . for what? His fingers disappeared inside her cunt-lips, and Alex gasped as they began to rub furiously at her clitoris.

Carter sang out his joy, as his semen spurted into Alex's backside – and she joined him in his song, her cunt dissolving into delicious spasms which left her gasping on the bed, her face pressed close against Madelon's firm white buttocks.

The Lord Chancellor paced up and down the polished marble floor of the throne room.

'Only one more trial to go,' he said. 'And if it, too, proves inconclusive, what are we to do then? I am an old man. I have no desire to remain as Regent for the rest of my days. And we cannot have two Crown Princes!'

Baron Mannhäuser, a wizened old man who had in his youth enjoyed a reputation as the best fucker in all Friedenheim, looked up from the council table.

'I have an idea, my Lord,' he said. 'It may perhaps allow us to solve the mystery once and for all.'

All eyes were on the Baron. Could he really solve this mystery which had brought such damaging uncertainty to the Principality?

'Years ago,' he continued, 'when I was in my prime and just before one of the Princes was abducted, I used to have a rather pleasing mistress. A true mistress of buggery and fellation, she was; and we spent many delightful hours together. Such wonderful, heavy breasts, so full of milk . . . Anyway, this lady, who was called Maria Dressler, was wet-nurse to the young princes. She left the castle when Albrecht was a small boy, and I think she went back to her family's farm in Lensburg. If you want to know more about the princes, Maria Dressler should be brought to the Castle. For she knows more about them than any person alive. She is our last hope of solving this mystery, once and for all.'

'Mr Carter is such a gentleman,' observed Madelon the following morning, as Alex brushed her long black hair and plaited it with fresh flowers. 'He fucks like an angel. It was so delightful to watch you two enjoying yourselves – what a dark horse you are, Alex!'

Alex blushed and paused for a moment in her brushing.

'I don't suppose he's half as impressed with me as I am with him,' she scoffed. 'Besides which, as soon as the wedding and coronation are over, he's sure to want to go back to England.' She turned the tables on her friend. 'What about your friend Dieter, Madelon? You've been seeing an awful lot of each other recently. What does Prince Albrecht have to say about that? Is Dieter going to be your official love once you are crowned?'

Madelon did not have time to think of a suitable reply, as at that moment the sounds of a great commotion floated in through the open window.

Dropping her silver-backed brush, Alex bounded over to peer down into the gardens below.

'There's a big group of people out there, in the rose gardens,' she announced breathlessly. 'They're standing in the shade of the pavilion, just beside the fountain. They're a little distance away, but I can see the Lord Chancellor, and the Privy Councillors, and some of the tutors from the Conservatoire . . . there's Mademoiselle Julienne, and Khara, and Signora Delmonico . . . and there are the two princes! They look so handsome – they're naked underneath their cloaks . . . such lovely cocks they have! Oh, do come and see, Madelon!'

Madelon was soon by her side, and they settled down on the window-seat, craning their necks to see what was going on in the rose garden.

'It must be the last of the trials,' explained Madelon. 'The trial of taste and abundance.'

As they watched, two guards came forwards into the rose garden, bearing two silver chalices which they laid at the feet of the two Princes. Albrecht and Reinholdt bowed and took off their silk cloaks – scarlet for Reinholdt and purple for Albrecht – revealing their handsome nakedness beneath. They both seemed every inch the prince . . .

'What is happening, Madelon? I don't quite understand.' Alex turned to her friend for enlightenment.

'This trial is based on an ancient Friedenbourgian

fertility rite,' explained Madelon, unbuttoning her robe and slipping it from her shoulders. She began to stroke her breasts, the better to enjoy the visual delights that the trial might have to offer. 'Each year, on the eve of the summer solstice, the Crown Prince must publicly present his Princess with a silver goblet filled with his own semen, which he has produced within the previous four hours. In this trial, each Prince must produce as much semen as he can within one hour, and the different levels will be measured in the silver chalices you can see down there, by the fountain. But that is not the end of the trial. Besides quantity, the ladies of the Conservatoire will also judge the quality of the Princes' semen, tasting it and evaluating its strength and potency.'

She helped Alex off with her dress, and they sat curled up together on the window-seat, caressing each other's bodies lightly as they peered out through the casement window.

Reinholdt and Albrecht were sitting side by side on the carved marble bench beside the fountain, and the Indian twins Ana and Meena, two expert fellatrices from the Conservatoire, were kneeling between their parted thighs, sucking them off and caressing their balls.

Prince Reinholdt was not long in reaching his climax, silently pulling his cock out of the girl's mouth, and watching with satisfaction as his semen spurted abundantly into the silver chalice held by Mademoiselle Julienne. Albrecht took longer, but it was evident from the admiring glances of those who stood around him that his pearly tribute was even more abundant than his brother's.

Exchanging excited glances, the two girls huddled

together, their fingers exploring each other's cunts now, like innocent yet lascivious children, taking their pleasure from what they saw and what they felt.

Next, the brothers approached the two girls, who had lain down on the gravel path which lined the rose borders. Madelon felt a thrill of fascinated horror as she thought of the delightful discomfort of being fucked on a hard gravel path . . . the pressure of each individual sharp stone, gnawing at her flesh whilst her lover toiled away on her belly, grinding her soft white buttocks further into the unforgiving gravel . . .

The Princes fucked as though their lives depended on it, for this was a race not to pleasure, but to abundance. Albrecht and Reinholdt seemed to pay little heed to the piteous groaning of the young girls beneath them, their bodies cruelly bruised and pierced by the sharp stones under their delicate flesh. They withdrew and spurted out their seed almost simultaneously, and the judges collected it meticulously in the two silver chalices.

As the Princes hauled the weeping girls to their feet and fell to buggering them on the soft green grass, Madelon and Alex rubbed each other's clitties with increasing enthusiasm, their own desires inflamed by these scenes of cold-hearted fucking.

The Princes fucked their partners again and again. They made a fine, princely show, but each time the jet of semen became thinner, sparser. Eventually, all they could do was slump onto the bench in exhaustion, and allow themselves to be wanked slowly to orgasm.

Madelon felt her own climax approaching and rubbed still harder at Alex's clitty, anxious that she should share her pleasure. With mingled cries of joy, they clung together as their cunts spasmed and the love-juice trickled down their thighs.

So wrapped up in their pleasure were they, that they hardly noticed that the fucking had come to an end, and that the judges, having measured the quantities of semen in the chalice, were about to proceed to the tasting.

'Look!' exclaimed Alex, drawing away from Madelon's embrace to peer out of the window once again. 'The judges are drinking down the Princes' semen.'

They watched as the tasting proceeded, as carefully as if the judges had been assessing a fine wine, whilst the princes looked on, exhausted and anxious. The judges fell to talking amongst themselves.

Eventually they called over the Lord Chancellor to hear their verdict. He shook his head and seemed distressed. What was going on? Had the contest at last produced a victor?

Nothing happened for what seemed a very long time; and then a single guardsman emerged from the group, grim-faced with determination, and began to walk slowly towards the Castle.

'Quick, get dressed!' exclaimed Madelon, pulling on her gown with unusual haste. 'It's Captain Tarnheim, and he's coming up here, to tell us the result!'

10 Discovery

Captain Tarnheim bowed low before Madelon; and she smiled to herself as she remembered how little respect he had shown her the last time they met. Her backside smarted still from the bite of his sword, and the wounds inflicted by the sharp birch twigs he had thrust into the depths of her delicate flesh.

Even now, as he bowed respectfully before her, she was aware of the Captain's eyes, never straying far from the fertile swell of her bosom, so imperfectly covered by her thin silk gown. She wondered if he too was remembering that afternoon in the forest, when he had both humiliated and pleasured her with his cruelty. And did he realise that, in forcing her to submit to his pleasure, he had also admitted to his one, terrible weakness? She was now the powerful one; for she knew his secret. Never again would he be free of the need, the hunger to possess her. A hunger which might never again be satisfied if she did not wish it . . .

'Madam,' he began. 'I come with news of the trials.'

'They have at last reached their outcome, Captain?'

'Alas, Madam, the judges cannot come to any decision, for the merits of Prince Reinholdt and

Prince Albrecht are so equal as to be indivisible; and there can therefore be no victor in the trials.'

'Then what is to be done? What will happen to the royal house of von Frieden? And what will happen to me . . . ?'

'Madam, another way has been found to resolve the dispute; but it requires your close co-operation. I have orders to bring you immediately before the Lord Chancellor. He awaits your presence at the pavilion, in the rose garden.'

'Then I shall come immediately.' Madelon smiled, a wicked smile. 'For who would dare defy the wishes of the Lord Chancellor?'

The Princes were still slumped, exhausted and defeated, on the marble bench, whilst their all-forgiving victims were soothing their abused pricks with cooling ointments. Madelon noticed a buxom, middle-aged countrywoman standing beside the Lord Chancellor and looking rather out of place at this ceremonial gathering. She couldn't help noticing that the Lord Chancellor seemed to be deriving great enjoyment from fondling the woman's massive breasts.

Florence, meanwhile, was as ever at Reinholdt's side, assiduously massaging his testicles with her dainty little fingers. Madelon caught her eye but Florence quickly looked away, an expression of suppressed rage and resentment darkening her pretty face.

Madelon curtseyed before the Lord Chancellor.

'You required my presence here, my Lord?'

He nodded, and indicated that she should dispense with the formalities.

'There is no need to kneel, my dear. I am glad that

you have come with such haste, for your assistance is most urgently required. It seems that, taking their individual merits into consideration, there is truly nothing to choose between Prince Albrecht and Prince Reinholdt. The judges have made their pronouncements, and the trials have resolved nothing. Both claimants have shown themselves worthy of princely honours, and yet neither has outdone the other.'

Seeing Madelon's concerned expression, he reassured her: 'Fortunately, our good friend Baron Mannhäuser has come to our rescue. It transpires that in his youth, the Baron was the intimate friend of Maria Dressler, the Princes' wet-nurse; and he wisely suggested that we should bring her here, since she was present at the Princes' birth, and knows them more intimately than any other. If anyone can determine which is the elder, it is she.

'I have interviewed Frau Dressler, and she has told me all that she knows of the Princes. Indeed, she has confirmed to me that there is one significant physical difference between the two Princes. Since you have been fairly and freely chosen as Crown Princess Elect, I now require you to perform an intimate examination of both Princes, and then return to me within the hour, to tell me which of the Princes is the true heir to the throne.'

Madelon looked at him in puzzlement.

'Am I not to have any idea of what I am looking for? How shall I know when I have found this "difference"?'

'None. I must not prejudice your findings in any way. Take each prince into the pavilion in turn, and examine him intimately. You will know when you have found the sign. That is all I can tell you. You

188

may go now, my dear; and may skill and instinct guide you to the truth.'

Madelon led Albrecht into the cool of the pavilion.

'Have you any idea what I'm looking for?' she asked him, once they were inside.

He shook his head, clearly quite baffled.

'I'm afraid I haven't the faintest idea, Madelon. Ah well, I suppose I shall just have to submit to your tender mercies . . . !'

Madelon was determined to carry out her duties conscientiously, for after all, the fate of the entire principality rested on her young shoulders. It was a tremendous responsibility for a young girl to bear. And yet it was so very difficult to concentrate with Albrecht's playful attentions constantly distracting her . . .

'Oh Albrecht, please behave,' she protested, as she tried desperately to examine his penis and testicles. But Albrecht would not behave . . . He grabbed hold of her and threw her backwards on to the floor, pulling up her skirt and pressing his burgeoning hardness against her belly.

'I . . . I thought you were exhausted, Albrecht,' panted Madelon, giggling in spite of herself. 'Surely there is no no spunk left in you, no stiffness left in your cock!'

'Not too tired to fuck you, my little princess! Why, it has been so long since you lay in my bed and let me stick my cock into you . . . ! Is your crack still tight and wet, or has it healed up without my cock to plough your furrow?'

Madelon felt her resistance melting away as Albrecht parted her thighs and felt for her diamond clittyring. He gave it a little twist, sending her into the most delicious spasms of pleasure. And, whilst she was gasping for breath, Albrecht took hold of his penis and directed it to her dripping wet hole.

She submitted to him with guilty joy, responding to each thrust of his pelvis with her own welcoming surge of lust. And they soon came together, soiling the dusty floor of the pavilion.

Madelon at last managed to perform her duties on Albrecht, but not a single distinguishing mark could she find, no matter how hard she looked.

Reinholdt was more than happy to enter the pavilion with Madelon; and his hand was on her backside almost before they had got through the door.

'My dear Madelon,' he breathed, as she parted his buttocks and inspected his arsehole. 'I've waited so long to be alone with you. Florence is a fine young woman, really quite gifted in the ways of lust, but you are a true princess among women. Make me Crown Prince of Friedenbourg, and I shall delight in bedding you on our wedding night.'

Madelon's determination to resist his advances simply melted away as Reinholdt's strong hands unbuttoned her blouse and took out her breasts, one at a time and delicately, as though handling some rare and delicate fledgling.

'You have magnificent titties,' he breathed; and took Madelon's left nipple into his mouth, sucking hard on it like a greedy baby. The blue-veined, creamy-white flesh of her breasts responded instantly to his touch, tensing and firming under his hands.

Before she knew it, Madelon was in strong arms. Her feet were leaving the ground, and she was sinking down, down, down, until at last she lay on the dusty ground, once again ready and willing to welcome in her lover. And Reinholdt's bold fingers were probing her flesh, sliding into her willing cunt . . .

'So!' he cried in mock outrage, scooping up some of the semen still oozing out of Madelon's cunt. 'Must my brother always be first in everything? Ah well; he has at least opened up the way for me . . .'

Reinholdt rammed into her eagerly and fucked with princely authority, almost commanding Madelon to join him in his orgasm. The base of his penis ground savagely against her clitty-ring, awakening waves of lust which made her clutch desperately at her lover's buttocks, urging him to ride her faster, faster, harder still . . . until the mad chase ended in a pearly spray of semen and a deluge of cunt-juice.

'Now, my sweet little Princess,' Reinholdt breathed in her ear. 'Won't you be a good girl and tell the Lord Chancellor that Reinholdt is the true heir to the throne of Friedenbourg?'

'I'm sorry, Reinholdt,' panted Madelon, her head still spinning in the afterglow of passion. 'But I can't resort to dishonesty, however tempted I might be. Now lie still, please, and let me examine you properly . . .'

As Madelon emerged from the pavilion, she saw that the Lord Chancellor and the Council of Ministers were still there, in the shade of the pavilion, waiting in suspense for their emissary to deliver her verdict. Albrecht and Reinholdt cast suspicious glances at each other as Madelon stepped forward and curtseyed.

'I am sorry, my Lord,' she said, finally. 'But I could find nothing – no distinguishing marks at all. In fact, if you had told me that Albrecht was Reinholdt, and Reinholdt was Albrecht, I could not have gainsaid you.'

A grim silence descended over the assembled throng.

'But that's impossible!' exclaimed the Lord Chancellor. 'Are you sure you looked properly?'

'Of course I did,' replied Madelon, indignantly. 'I am a prefect of the Conservatoire, not some timid virgin!'

The Chancellor turned to Maria Dressler and demanded:

'Have you lied to me, madam?'

The poor woman immediately burst into tears.

'Indeed no, my Lord! Why would I do such a terrible thing? You know that I am devoted to the Royal Family of Friedenbourg. I told you about the birthmark, and it was true. The elder of the children had a tiny, heart-shaped birthmark underneath his foreskin! I can't see how it can have disappeared!'

The Lord Chancellor turned to Madelon again.

'You checked carefully underneath their foreskins?'

Madelon nodded. 'Of course.' But her thoughts were elsewhere. 'Did you say . . . a birthmark underneath the foreskin? A little heart-shaped birthmark? On the underside of the penis?'

'Yes, but I didn't say it was on the underside . . . How did you guess? And where are you going, Madelon?'

Madelon bobbed a hasty curtsey, took to her heels and fled. As she ran, she called back over her shoulder:

'Please wait. I won't be very long. I think I can solve this mystery for you, once and for all . . .'

The scullery-maid lifted up her skirts to reveal a pair of starched white bloomers, slit open at the crotch as was the custom among many of Friedenbourg's northern peasants. Her dark-brown pubic hair showed invitingly through the crack, forming a tantalising contrast to the sparkling white of her bloomers.

'Why, Herr Richtig, sir, you're looking awful down. Would a fuck cheer you up, perhaps?'

Dieter smiled at her, appreciating her kindness. He didn't really feel much inclined to fuck the lass, but she was so good-hearted . . . how could he refuse? She would be so hurt and disappointed if he turned her down.

He unfastened his belt, and pulled down his corduroy breeches, revealing his handsome prick.

'Why, sir, you're not quite stiff yet. Let me help you . . .'

Gerda got down on her knees and gaily began to suck at Dieter's prick, so enthusiastically and expertly that his sorrows lightened and he began to grow stiff and eager for her.

When he was good and hard, she bent forward, supporting her floury hands on the wooden workbench, and gathering her skirts above her waist.

Dieter penetrated her easily, for her cunt was generously proportioned and well lubricated.

'That's it, dear sir; ram it in to me nice and hard, for I do so love a good hard fucking. And afterwards, perhaps you would like to bugger me? Old Tom the gardener tells me I've a nice tight arse. Or maybe you'd like to stick your cock between my tits, and I'll squeeze them tight about you, to give you something a little different, like . . . ?'

Dieter abandoned himself to the pure pleasure of

these few moments, to the mindless, rhythmic slide of cock into cunt. Gerda was a good fuck . . . but she wasn't Madelon. Dieter was worried about her. What if she was still in pain after her ordeal in the forest? And when was he going to see her again? Would she still have time for him when she was Crown Princess of Friedenbourg?

His orgasm crept up on him almost out of the blue, and he clutched at Gerda's friendly breasts as his semen spurted into her cunt.

He was just thanking Gerda and wiping his prick before putting it back into his breeches, when the kitchen door burst open and in rushed Madelon, gasping for breath.

'Dieter, Dieter, come quickly! There's no time for fucking: it's a matter of life or death!' she exclaimed, grabbing his hand and dragging him towards the door.

'What . . . ? I don't understand!' replied Dieter, still trying to fasten his belt. 'Where are you taking me?'

'To the rose garden! There's not a moment to lose!'

And they raced off together down the path to the rose garden, whilst Gerda stared after them in blank incomprehension.

The Lord Chancellor and his entourage watched open-mouthed as Madelon came racing down the path towards them, dragging a bemused Dieter by the hand.

'What on earth do you mean, young lady, by bringing one of the castle grooms into the middle of an important matter of State?' demanded Reinholdt, getting angrily to his feet.

'Let her speak,' replied the Lord Chancellor, sternly. 'Now, my dear, what have you to say for yourself, and what is the meaning of all this?'

Madelon gently pushed Dieter forwards.

'It is quite simple,' she replied. 'This is your Prince. Dieter is the missing heir to the throne of Friedenbourg!'

After a brief and shocked silence, the assembled throng dissolved into fits of derisive laughter.

Madelon blushed crimson with anger. Soon they would be laughing on the other side of their faces. Deftly, she unfastened Dieter's belt and fly-buttons, pulled out his prick and began to masturbate it.

In spite of his confusion and embarrassment, Dieter began to respond to her expert touch, and his penis swelled impressively in Madelon's hand. Gently, she peeled back the foreskin and turned in triumph to the Lord Chancellor.

'My Lord,' she said, 'I think you will find this sufficient proof.'

11　The Prince

The Lord Chancellor stared in disbelief at the birth-mark on Dieter's penis. There was no mistaking it: it was small, red, heart-shaped . . . there could not be two birthmarks like it in the world, let alone in Friedenbourg. He beckoned to Frau Dressler to come and look.

'Is that the birthmark?' he demanded. 'The royal birthmark you saw on the elder Prince's penis?'

With a cry of joy, Frau Dressler fell to her knees, weeping copiously and showering Dieter's penis with kisses.

'My Prince!' she cried. 'At last you are returned to me! My own darling little Prince! I feared we had lost you forever!'

Albrecht and Reinholdt stared at each other, their faces quite drained of colour.

'But how can this youth be a Prince?' demanded Albrecht.

'He is just a humble stable-lad!' scoffed Reinholdt, his expression hovering uncertainly between derision and doubt, and his voice full of resentment.

Baron Mannhäuser got unsteadily to his feet and tottered forward, leaning heavily on his stick.

'According to the testimony of Frau Dressler, this seems indeed to be the birthmark,' he concluded, peering at it intently through his pince-nez. 'But how can this young fellow be a prince, since, quite apart from his lowly station in life, he has no twin brother? The kidnapped prince was a twin, and it is plain to see that Dieter is no kin to Reinholdt or Albrecht.'

Frau Dressler clutched the Baron's hand, as though beseeching forgiveness.

'Oh dear sir,' she sighed. 'I fear it is all my fault that this terrible confusion has happened. You see, at the time when the royal babes were born, my unmarried sister was also due to give birth. Having some influence at the Castle, and not wishing her to give birth in poverty, I arranged for her to come into my private apartments at the Castle. All went well, and both mothers gave birth to healthy twin boys.

'Well, all four little boys were adorable – dark-haired little mites with blue eyes – and I must admit I feared I might mix them up . . . One night, when all four children had been put to bed by an under-maid, I returned to find them all asleep in their cots in the royal nursery. I confess, I was much confused, for they were all very alike. But – God forgive me! – I believed that the under-maid had returned the babies to the right mothers, and I thought no more about it. At the end of a week, my sister went home to the village with her twins, and the two princes were brought up at Castle Amor.

'I was devastated, of course, when one of the princes was stolen away, and I knew it must have been the elder of the children, for when I checked the remaining child, he had no birthmark under his foreskin. I never thought for a moment that perhaps my sister was looking after the two true princes.'

The Lord Chancellor turned to Dieter.

'This does not solve the essential problem. Tell me, Herr Richtig. Have you a twin brother?'

'I have indeed, my Lord, though he is a quiet lad, and not known at the Castle, for he never leaves his village except to go to market. His name is Karel, and he has a little farm near to the Austrian border. But what does all of this mean, my Lord . . . ?'

The Lord Chancellor extended his hand to Dieter, and then fell to his knees before him.

'My dear Sir, do not look so perplexed. There is no mystery about it. It means that you are the true heir to the throne of Friedenbourg!'

Crown Prince Dieter of Friedenbourg sat in the throne room at Castle Amor, idly stroking his Princess's delectable thighs through the thin, silky fabric of her gown. She turned to him and smiled, a glorious smile full of mischief and lust.

'Shall we fuck, Dieter? I long to pleasure you again with my lips and tongue and cunt and arse . . .'

Dieter kissed her passionately, rubbing the hardening tips of her beautiful breasts. Madelon made a wonderful Crown Princess. They had hardly stopped fucking since the coronation, and together they did admirable honour to Friedenbourg's traditions of sexual delight.

'Patience, my love,' he breathed. 'We shall fuck again very soon. This afternoon, we shall spend in the Garden of Earthly Delights; and later we shall perhaps return to the stables where we first enjoyed the bounty of each other's bodies. And as for this evening, we shall invite Alex and Mr Carter to join us in our bedchamber, in celebration of their forthcoming marriage.

'But first, I must do something I have meant to

do ever since I found out who I really was. I must help those poor fellows Albrecht and Reinholdt. There must be something I can do to ease their lot – for it must be terrible for them to have been dispossessed of everything they have ever hoped for. But what can I do? What ought I to do to help them, Madelon?'

Madelon put her arms round his neck and whispered playfully in his ear.

'I think I have the answer, my sweet. But first, you must lick out my cunt, or I shan't tell it to you . . .'

Count Albrecht von Heller and Count Reinholdt von Niedermayer were no longer displeased with the quality of their existence. Their recent ennoblement by Prince Dieter had come as a pleasant surprise, equalled only by the rather generous settlement upon each of them of one hundred thousand crowns per year, for life.

But perhaps the best surprise of all had been thought up by Princess Madelon, that clever girl. It seemed that they had underestimated her resourcefulness. For she had soon guessed that such talented and refined young men would not wish to remain idle for long. No, they must be found some noble and congenial occupation which would make full use of the dazzling range of their gifts.

And so it was that Count Reinholdt and Count Albrecht were appointed honorary vice-principals of the Conservatoire of Delicate Arts.

One fine September morning after breakfast, Reinholdt gave Florence's pert little titties a final squeeze and then left his apartments to stroll across the lawns to the main Conservatoire buildings, hands in his pockets and humming a bawdy song.

He found Albrecht already hard at work in his classroom, introducing himself to the latest intake of pupils: twenty-four of the most delectable, refined, willing and lustful young ladies in Europe.

'Good morning, brother!' he hailed him. 'Working hard?'

Albrecht nodded. 'There are two succulent virgins in this class, too,' he added with a lecherous smile. 'I shall be initiating them in my rooms this afternoon. I have such a busy timetable . . . I don't suppose I could persuade you to share in the onerous duty?'

Surveying Albrecht's class of eager young ladies, Reinholdt could not help agreeing that, whilst power might have once had its attractions, pleasure had even more. Dieter and Madelon were welcome to the throne of Friedenbourg, and all it entailed. All in all, they had definitely got the better of the deal.

Letter from Esme

Dear Readers

Another month, another letter. I'm writing this in November, in the midst of shortening days, falling leaves, and urchins begging for fireworks money. And thanks to the miracles of modern book production, you're reading this next Spring, or sometime thereafter, and dreary Winter is already a memory. It's rather like time travel, isn't it?

Now I must tell you about the Nexus books that are being published in March 1993, and in the back of one of which you've found this little message.

Stephanie's Revenge and *Castle Amor* are the brand new novels; *A Man with a Maid 3* is the classic reprint. Which one have you got your fingers into?

Stephanie has come a long way since we first met her as an ordinary but increasingly sex-obsessed working girl in the book called *Stephanie*. In *Stephanie's Castle* she discovered the mingled pleasures and pains of the high life in an Italian castle with a very interesting set of cellars. Now, in *Stephanie's Revenge*, she plays tit for tat with an Italian gangster. I won't spoil your fun by telling you who wins in the end, but I can assure you there's plenty more of that delicious mingling along the way.

Castle Amor is a much more light-hearted affair. It's excellent bed-time reading, and one way or another it'll send you off to sleep with a smile on your face. Completely silly, but wittily written, fast-paced, and chock full of well-bred young ladies throwing off their crinolines and having fun with stable boys. I won't give away the plot, but if I were to say nineteenth century, middle of Europe, small principality overburdened with randy aristos, and *The Prisoner of Zenda*, I'm sure you'd get the idea.

A Man with a Maid 3 is, of course, the third volume of a trilogy. Yes, I know I'm stating the obvious, but anyway: if you like it, go and look for the previous two books — new editions have only just been published. I'm not sure just how much of the trilogy is authentically Victorian and how much is more recent, but it remains one of my favourite Olde English reads. The third book sends me quite weak at the knees with indecision: should I identify with the gorgeous and severe Helen Hotspur, or with one of the thoroughly chastised young women who endure and enjoy punishment at Helen's hands in the sound-proofed privacy of the Snuggery?

Coming along next month we have: *Ms Deedes on Paradise Island*, in which the lovely Ella investigates a particularly nasty trade in aphrodisiacs; *Obsession*, the third book by Maria del Rey, author of *The Institute* and *Paradise Bay* — another very different story, but once again very powerful; and the classic reprint is *Violette*, real French naughtiness from the nineteenth century.

Sometimes I am asked, 'Esme, how did a gentle, sweet, innocent, beautiful flower such as you become involved in the seedy world of smutty books?' Actually that's not true: I made it up because I want to talk about where Nexus authors come from.

It's not a seedy world, actually. The people at Nexus are young, very friendly, very open about erotic writing, and work in light and airy modern offices on Ladbroke Grove. It must come as a surprise to anyone who expects to find a team of scruffy old men in dirty raincoats leering over page 3 girls in a dark East End warehouse.

And the people who write Nexus books are surprising, too: they're so downright ordinary. I've bumped into some of them at the Nexus office, and honestly, you wouldn't be able to tell them from a bunch of teachers, accountants, and housewives. Because that's exactly what they are! Not all of them, of course: some make all of their living from writing, and one or two of these are quite well-known, and write under pseudonyms.

And although many of them look ordinary, they're not, of course. Because unlike so many people, who gleefully read every tiny detail of the tabloids' reports about awful rape cases and books by Madonna but moan about declining moral standards and inadequate obscenity laws, Nexus authors aren't hypocritical about sex. We all do it, we all like it, and we all enjoy reading about it. More power to their elbows, say I.

And how do you become one of this select band of literary convention-busters? You do what I did: send a letter and a large, stamped, self-addressed envelope to the Nexus office, and they will send you a copy of their guidelines for prospective authors. This document is more than a tip sheet: it contains everything you need to know — how to present your work, what kinds of stories are acceptable, how much material to send in for consideration. If you have any questions, the Nexus editors are happy to answer specific enquiries by phone.

I've been looking at the latest version of the guidelines. Here are a few tips that might save you some time and trouble if you're thinking about having a go at writing for Nexus.

A few subjects, not surprisingly, are completely unacceptable: sex involving children or animals, for instance. The editors say that they are increasingly wary of stories that even hint at underage sex; they advise authors that all the characters in a Nexus book should be adults, and that if any character appears childish, or in a situation where you might expect to find a child, the author should make it unmistakably clear that the character is over sixteen years old *at least*. For the same reason, stories which include incest are unlikely to find favour.

There's not much point sending in a short story: Nexus books are full-length novels, and a short story will give the editors only the vaguest of ideas about your ability to write a novel.

And the standard of presentation is important: a story produced with a rickety old typewriter with uneven keys and a fading ribbon on dog-eared paper will not impress as much as a story laser-printed on to fresh white pages. It's not just that the latter is easier to read: it also suggests that the author is a professional writer who takes his writing seriously.

Finally, when you've written your piece, jiffy-bagged it and consigned it to the post, don't expect a quick answer. Sometimes (the editors claim) unsolicited typescripts (see, I'm learning technical terms!) are read and returned within a few days. But sometimes a backlog develops, and it takes months. Patiently waiting for publishers is one of the necessary disciplines of being an author, it seems. And one of the less pleasant ones!

That's about it for this month. I'd like to know what you'd like to know about Nexus, so please write in and tell me what I can do for you!

But remember — I'm writing these letters six months in advance, so you won't notice any changes for some time. My response is going to be unusually slow!

And don't, whatever you do, send me anonymous letters full of your wild sexual fantasies. Any such letters will (after I've read them, of course) be turned over the the Nexus editors and made into a book. Well, maybe. So there!

THE BEST IN EROTIC READING – BY POST

The Nexus Library of Erotica – almost one hundred and fifty volumes – is available from many booksellers and newsagents. If you have any difficulty obtaining the books you require, you can order them by post. Photocopy the list below, or tear the list out of the book; then tick the titles you want and fill in the form at the end of the list. Titles marked 1993 are not yet available: please do not try to order them – just look out for them in the shops!

CONTEMPORARY EROTICA

AMAZONS	Erin Caine	£3.99	
COCKTAILS	Stanley Carten	£3.99	
CITY OF ONE-NIGHT STANDS	Stanley Carten	£4.50	
CONTOURS OF DARKNESS	Marco Vassi	£4.99	
THE GENTLE DEGENERATES	Marco Vassi	£4.99	
MIND BLOWER	Marco Vassi	£4.99	
THE SALINE SOLUTION	Marco Vassi	£4.99	
DARK FANTASIES	Nigel Anthony	£4.99	
THE DAYS AND NIGHTS OF MIGUMI	P.M.	£4.50	
THE LATIN LOVER	P.M.	£3.99	
THE DEVIL'S ADVOCATE	Anonymous	£4.50	
DIPLOMATIC SECRETS	Antoine Lelouche	£3.50	
DIPLOMATIC PLEASURES	Antoine Lelouche	£3.50	
DIPLOMATIC DIVERSIONS	Antoine Lelouche	£4.50	
ENGINE OF DESIRE	Alexis Arven	£3.99	
DIRTY WORK	Alexis Arven	£3.99	
DREAMS OF FAIR WOMEN	Celeste Arden	£2.99	
THE FANTASY HUNTERS	Celeste Arden	£3.99	
A GALLERY OF NUDES	Anthony Grey	£3.99	
THE GIRL FROM PAGE 3	Mike Angelo	£3.99	
HELEN – A MODERN ODALISQUE	James Stern	£4.99	1993
HOT HOLLYWOOD NIGHTS	Nigel Anthony	£4.50	
THE INSTITUTE	Maria del Ray	£4.99	

LAURE-ANNE	Laure-Anne	£4.50	
LAURE-ANNE ENCORE	Laure-Anne	£4.99	
LAURE-ANNE TOUJOURS	Laure-Anne	£4.99	
A MISSION FOR Ms DEEDS	Carole Andrews	£4.99	1993
Ms DEEDES AT HOME	Carole Andrews	£4.50	
Ms DEEDES ON PARADISE ISLAND	Carole Andrews	£4.99	1993
MY SEX MY SOUL	Amelia Greene	£2.99	
OBSESSION	Maria del Rey	£4.99	1993
ONE WEEK IN THE PRIVATE HOUSE	Esme Ombreux	£4.50	
PALACE OF FANTASIES	Delver Maddingley	£4.99	
PALACE OF SWEETHEARTS	Delver Maddingley	£4.99	1993
PARADISE BAY	Maria del Rey	£4.50	
QUEENIE AND CO	Francesca Jones	£4.99	1993
QUEENIE AND CO IN JAPAN	Francesca Jones	£4.99	1993
QUEENIE AND CO IN ARGENTINA	Francesca Jones	£4.99	1993
THE SECRET WEB	Jane-Anne Roberts	£3.99	
SECRETS LIE ON PILLOWS	James Arbroath	£4.50	
SECRETS IN SUMATRA	James Arbroath	£4.99	1993
STEPHANIE	Susanna Hughes	£4.50	
STEPHANIE'S CASTLE	Susanna Hughes	£4.50	
STEPHENIE'S DOMAIN	Susanna Hughes	£4.99	1993
STEPHANIE'S REVENGE	Susanna Hughes	£4.99	1993
THE DOMINO TATTOO	Cyrian Amberlake	£4.50	
THE DOMINO ENIGMA	Cyrian Amberlake	£3.99	
THE DOMINO QUEEN	Cyrian Amberlake	£4.99	

EROTIC SCIENCE FICTION

ADVENTURES IN THE PLEASURE ZONE	Delaney Silver	£4.99	
EROGINA	Christopher Denham	£4.50	
HARD DRIVE	Stanley Carten	£4.99	
PLEASUREHOUSE 13	Agnetha Anders	£3.99	
LAST DAYS OF THE PLEASUREHOUSE	Agnetha Anders	£4.50	
TO PARADISE AND BACK	D.H.Master	£4.50	
WICKED	Andrea Arven	£3.99	
WILD	Andrea Arven	£4.50	

ANCIENT & FANTASY SETTINGS

CHAMPIONS OF LOVE	Anonymous	£3.99	
CHAMPIONS OF DESIRE	Anonymous	£3.99	

CHAMPIONS OF PLEASURE	Anonymous	£3.50	
THE SLAVE OF LIDIR	Aran Ashe	£4.50	
THE FOREST OF BONDAGE	Aran Ashe	£4.50	
KNIGHTS OF PLEASURE	Erin Caine	£4.50	
PLEASURE ISLAND	Aran Ashe	£4.99	
ROMAN ORGY	Marcus van Heller	£4.50	

EDWARDIAN, VICTORIAN & OLDER EROTICA

ADVENTURES OF A SCHOOLBOY	Anonymous	£3.99	
THE AUTOBIOGRAPHY OF A FLEA	Anonymous	£2.99	
BEATRICE	Anonymous	£3.99	
THE BOUDOIR	Anonymous	£3.99	
CASTLE AMOR	Erin Caine	£4.99	1993
CHOOSING LOVERS FOR JUSTINE	Aran Ashe	£4.99	1993
THE DIARY OF A CHAMBERMAID	Mirabeau	£2.99	
THE LIFTED CURTAIN	Mirabeau	£4.99	
EVELINE	Anonymous	£2.99	
MORE EVELINE	Anonymous	£3.99	
FESTIVAL OF VENUS	Anonymous	£4.50	
'FRANK' & I	Anonymous	£2.99	
GARDENS OF DESIRE	Roger Rougiere	£4.50	
OH, WICKED COUNTRY	Anonymous	£2.99	
LASCIVIOUS SCENES	Anonymous	£4.50	
THE LASCIVIOUS MONK	Anonymous	£4.50	
LAURA MIDDLETON	Anonymous	£3.99	
A MAN WITH A MAID 1	Anonymous	£4.99	
A MAN WITH A MAID 2	Anonymous	£4.99	
A MAN WITH A MAID 3	Anonymous	£4.99	
MAUDIE	Anonymous	£2.99	
THE MEMOIRS OF DOLLY MORTON	Anonymous	£4.50	
A NIGHT IN A MOORISH HAREM	Anonymous	£3.99	
PARISIAN FROLICS	Anonymous	£2.99	
PLEASURE BOUND	Anonymous	£3.99	
THE PLEASURES OF LOLOTTE	Andrea de Nerciat	£3.99	
THE PRIMA DONNA	Anonymous	£3.99	
RANDIANA	Anonymous	£4.50	
REGINE	E.K.	£2.99	

THE ROMANCE OF LUST 1	Anonymous	£3.99	
THE ROMANCE OF LUST 2	Anonymous	£2.99	
ROSA FIELDING	Anonymous	£2.99	
SUBURBAN SOULS 1	Anonymous	£2.99	
SURBURBAN SOULS 2	Anonymous	£3.99	
THREE TIMES A WOMAN	Anonymous	£2.99	
THE TWO SISTERS	Anonymous	£3.99	
VIOLETTE	Anonymous	£4.99	

"THE JAZZ AGE"

ALTAR OF VENUS	Anonymous	£3.99	
THE SECRET GARDEN ROOM	Georgette de la Tour	£3.50	
BEHIND THE BEADED CURTAIN	Georgette de la Tour	£3.50	
BLANCHE	Anonymous	£3.99	
BLUE ANGEL NIGHTS	Margaret von Falkensee	£4.99	
BLUE ANGEL DAYS	Margaret von Falkensee	£4.99	
BLUE ANGEL SECRETS	Margaret von Falkensee	£4.99	
CAROUSEL	Anonymous	£4.50	
CONFESSIONS OF AN ENGLISH MAID	Anonymous	£3.99	
FLOSSIE	Anonymous	£2.50	
SABINE	Anonymous	£3.99	
PLAISIR D'AMOUR	Anne-Marie Villefranche	£4.50	
FOLIES D'AMOUR	Anne-Marie Villefranche	£2.99	
JOIE D'AMOUR	Anne-Marie Villefranche	£3.99	
MYSTERE D'AMOUR	Anne-Marie Villefranche	£3.99	
SECRETS D'AMOUR	Anne-Marie Villefranche	£3.50	
SOUVENIR D'AMOUR	Anne-Marie Villefranche	£3.99	

WORLD WAR 2

SPIES IN SILK	Piers Falconer	£4.50	
WAR IN HIGH HEELS	Piers Falconer	£4.99	1993

CONTEMPORARY FRENCH EROTICA (translated into English)

EXPLOITS OF A YOUNG DON JUAN	Anonymous	£2.99	
INDISCREET MEMOIRS	Alain Dorval	£2.99	
INSTRUMENT OF PLEASURE	Celeste Piano	£4.50	
JOY	Joy Laurey	£2.99	
JOY AND JOAN	Joy Laurey	£2.99	

JOY IN LOVE	Joy Laurey	£2.75	
LILIANE	Paul Verguin	£3.50	
MANDOLINE	Anonymous	£3.99	
LUST IN PARIS	Antoine S.	£4.99	
NYMPH IN PARIS	Galia S.	£2.99	
SCARLET NIGHTS	Juan Muntaner	£3.99	
SENSUAL LIAISONS	Anonymous	£3.50	
SENSUAL SECRETS	Anonymous	£3.99	
THE NEW STORY OF O	Anonymous	£4.50	
THE IMAGE	Jean de Berg	£3.99	
VIRGINIE	Nathalie Perreau	£4.50	
THE PAPER WOMAN	Francois Rey	£4.50	

SAMPLERS & COLLECTIONS

EROTICON 1	ed. J-P Spencer	£4.50	
EROTICON 2	ed. J-P Spencer	£4.50	
EROTICON 3	ed. J-P Spencer	£4.50	
EROTICON 4	ed. J-P Spencer	£4.99	
NEW EROTICA 1	ed. Esme Ombreux	£4.99	
THE FIESTA LETTERS	ed. Chris Lloyd	£4.50	
THE PLEASURES OF LOVING	ed. Maren Sell	£3.99	

NON-FICTION

HOW TO DRIVE YOUR MAN WILD IN BED	Graham Masterton	£4.50	
HOW TO DRIVE YOUR WOMAN WILD IN BED	Graham Masterton	£3.99	
HOW TO BE THE PERFECT LOVER	Graham Masterton	£2.99	
FEMALE SEXUAL AWARENESS	Barry & Emily McCarthy	£5.99	
LINZI DREW'S PLEASURE GUIDE	Linzi Drew	£4.99	
LETTERS TO LINZI	Linzi Drew	£4.99	1993
WHAT MEN WANT	Susan Crain Bakos	£3.99	
YOUR SEXUAL SECRETS	Marty Klein	£3.99	

Please send me the books I have ticked above.

Name   . . . .
Address   . . . .

            . . . .

            . . . . Post code . . . .

Send to: **Nexus Books Cash Sales, PO Box 11, Falmouth, Cornwall, TR10 9EN**

Please enclose a cheque or postal order, made payable to **Nexus Books**, to the value of the books you have ordered plus postage and packing costs as follows:

UK and BFPO – £1.00 for the first book, 50p for the second book, and 30p for each subsequent book to a maximum of £3.00;

Overseas (including Republic of Ireland) – £2.00 for the first book, £1.00 for the second book, and 50p for each subsequent book.

If you would prefer to pay by VISA or ACCESS/MASTERCARD, please write your card number here:

— — — —   — — — —   — — — —   — — — —

Signature: _____